James Philip

FOOTBALL IN THE RUINS

The World Cup of 1966

A Timeline 10/27/62 Book

Cover concept by James Philip
Graphic Design by Beastleigh Web Design

_____

The Timeline 10/27/62 Series

Main Series
Book 1: Operation Anadyr
Book 2: Love is Strange
Book 3: The Pillars of Hercules
Book 4: Red Dawn
Book 5: The Burning Time
Book 6: Tales of Brave Ulysses
Book 7: A Line in the Sand
Book 8: The Mountains of the Moon
Book 9: All Along the Watchtower
Book 10: Crow on the Cradle
Book 11: 1966 & All That
Book 12:   Only in America
Book 13: Warsaw Concerto
Book 14: Eight Miles High
Book 15: Won't Get Fooled Again

Coming in 2021
Stumbling Towards the Edge
Book 16: Armadas
Book 17: Smoke on the Water
Book 18: Cassandra's Song

USA Series
Book 1: Aftermath
Book 2: California Dreaming
Book 3: The Great Society
Book 4: Ask Not of Your Country
Book 5: The American Dream

Australia Series
Book 1: Cricket on the Beach
Book 2: Operation Manna

———————

Check out the latest news about the
Timeline 10/27/62 Saga at
www.thetimelinesaga.com
and
The details of all my other books at
www.jamesphilip.co.uk

Contents

1 | Preface

When the representatives of sixty-nine national governing bodies of Association Football gathered in Rome a few days ahead of the start of the Football Tournament of the 1960 Summer Olympic Games – the normal governance and regulatory minutiae apart – there was only one real matter which excited more than passing interest within, or without the 32nd Congress of the Fédération Internationale de Football Association (FIFA); namely, the selection of the host nation for the 1966 World Cup.

FIFA had come a long way – albeit travelling a bumpy road – since the footballing tribes had first got together in 1904 when the national associations of Belgium, Denmark, France, Germany, Holland, Spain, represented by the Madrid Football Club, their national governing body not being established until 1913, Sweden and Switzerland had come together and all parties had agreed *in principle* that there needed to be a single authority to oversee the international game. This was a thing accomplished the 21st May of that year in a back room of the Union des Sociétés Françaises de Sports Athlétiques at the Rue Saint Honoré in Paris.

There has been debate ever since about whether Germany ought to be considered a 'founding member' since the German Football Association only declared its affiliation by telegram to the infant Fédération Internationale de Football Association *after* its birth. Needless to say, the country which claimed – legitimately – to have invented the game of soccer, England, had not bothered to turn up to the first 'Congress' in Paris. Thus, in the absence of the 'big beast' of football a twenty-eight-year old French journalist, Robert Guérin, the secretary of the Football Department of the Union des Sociétés Françaises de Sports Athlétiques, and therefore very much the man on the spot, was elected FIFA's first President.

It was only two years later at FIFA's third Congress in 1906 that Guerin was replaced by Daniel Burley Woodfall, the Football Association's man from Blackburn in England. Woodfall, eleven days short of his fifty-fourth birthday when he was elected on 4th June 1906 was a man on a mission, taking the reins determined to unify the rules of the game at the international level. The *Laws of the Game* drafted during his stewardship – based almost entirely on the English game – became mandatory. Subsequently, it was Woodfall who was to organise the first major international competition; that of the football tournament of the 1908 London Olympic Games.

When Woodfall had died whilst in office in 1918 a Dutch banker, Cornelis August Wilhelm Hirschman, the General Secretary of FIFA had stepped in, personally saving and financing the organisation, with Hirschmann's own company thereafter acting as the sole investment broker for FIFA and the Dutch Olympic Committee until it, in turn, was bankrupted by the 1929 Stock Market Crash, even after the election of Jules Rimet, for whom the trophy awarded to the winners of the World Cup would later be named, became President in 1921.

The first two World Wars of the twentieth century had inevitably caused rifts within FIFA with various warring parties coming and going in disgust, protest or under orders from their Governments but after 1945 things had settled down and by 1960 the organisation had sixty-nine full members. Although global representation was by no means comprehensive most regions were well represented; although the Europeans still held the whip hand in the most important decisions.

For example, when it came to selecting who should host World Cup Finals it was still the Europeans who called the shots; although not so much as even a decade before because Cold War politics often trumped all other sporting considerations. However, by 1960 there was a general understanding that FIFA's premier competition ought – all things being equal - to rotate from Europe to the rest of the World and back again in an eight-year cycle. Such was the footballing post-World War II settlement; competitions having been hosted by Brazil (in 1950), Switzerland (in 1954), the Swiss having first been nominated to host the World Cup in 1946, Sweden (in 1958) and scheduled to be held in Chile in June 1962.

The 32nd Congress of FIFA had been called to sit four days before the start of the Olympic Tournament. Given that 1966 was a 'European' year only three candidates had entered bids to host the 1966 tournament: England,

West Germany and Spain.

UEFA - the Union of European Football Associations – founded in Basel in 1954 theoretically controlled about half the votes in that Congress but like FIFA in its early years it often found it hard to speak, let alone act with a single voice. Therefore, there was no clear UEFA 'consensus' candidate in the election to host the 1966 World Cup, even though everybody agreed that on the face of it, England were the obvious favourites. In the end the Spanish dropped out of the race so as to not split the anti-English vote and it became a straight contest between the English and the West German Football Associations.

Inevitably, the English had more leverage and favours to call in than their West German opponents; and truthfully, there was an unspoken feeling abroad that perhaps, it was *England's Turn.* England won 34 votes; West Germany 27 and nobody cavilled at the process or the final decision. In fact, the following year, Sir Stanley Rous the great old man of the FA, at an 'extraordinary' Congress held in London called because of the death of his predecessor, Arthur Drewry in March 1961, became the 6th elected President of FIFA in a mood of positively ostentatious magnanimity that superficially united the footballing family.

FIFA had survived two World Wars, and schisms aplenty in its fifty-six-year history up until that 32nd Congress in Rome ahead of the 1960 Olympiad. However, nobody was to know that its decision that day in June would result in a World Cup tournament fought out in a World changed out of all recognition.

The World Cup of 1966 was forever to be remembered in legend as the time when 'football in the ruins' triumphed, albeit briefly, over the madness and mendacity of the princes who had wrecked the northern hemisphere that day in October 1962.

In retrospect we view those days through rose-tinted glasses; easily forgetting the circumstances in which that famous tournament was played; and how close it came to never happening at all. It would not, could not have happened but for the bloody-mindedness of several key participants in football and government but the honour and the glory belong, in toto, to the players, that band of heroes – and a few minor villains - who will live indelibly in the memories of the peoples of so many of the countries involved in that titanic struggle.

Yet even as late as the spring of 1965 the footballing world had assumed that, as in 1942 and 1946 that there would be no World Cup in 1966. The South Americans had discussed, among themselves the possibility of inviting Italy, Spain and Portugal to send teams to a 'Continental Cup' of some kind in the winter of 1966-67 to be held in either or both of Brazil and Argentina but nothing had come of this by the time the Football Association seriously contemplated exercising its 'right' to host the 1966 tournament in England.

Herein, the battles off as well as on the field form an intrinsic part of the broader narrative. International sport has never been, nor will it ever be, non-political. Sport is after all, like life; a stage upon which we as a species explore the best and the worst of ourselves and our opponents, gleaning lessons – hopefully - *without* spilling egregious amounts of blood in the process.

Sport is subtext, emotions, highs and lows of delight and despair and football has only been so universally successful because within its cut and thrust, blood and thunder lie tantalising subtlety, courage and possibilities that constantly astonish even the oldest of journalistic hacks, this author included.

So, live with me again the heady days of July 1966 when a nation finally began to throw off the nightmare of the October War; when after three years and over eight months of grief, hunger and unwanted foreign wars it rediscovered anew its true heart and voice.

This then is the story of *Football in the Ruins – the World Cup of 1966!*

M.J. Christopher
Garden City Press, New London
27th October 2016

2 | Chile - 1962

The last World Cup before the World cataclysm of October 1962 very nearly did not happen – or rather it very nearly did not happen in Chile – because of the *Terremoto de Valdivia* of 22nd May 1960. *The Great Chilean Earthquake* – one of a series of massive seismic events over a period of several weeks to strike the country, was then and remains the most powerful ever recorded; it struck at 15:11 local time and lasted for over ten minutes registering at its peak a magnitude in the vicinity of 9.5 on the Richter scale. Its epicentre was three hundred and fifty miles south of the capital city, Santiago; eighty feet high tsunami waves ravaged the Chilean coast, and more distantly waves of over thirty feet wrecked Hilo on the Hawaiian Islands and caused damage as far away as Japan, Australia, the Philippines and the Aleutians. It was a miracle that the death toll was less than ten thousand but afterwards, Chile, its infrastructure and its football stadiums were devastated.

Famously, Carlos Dittborn, President of the Chilean Organising Committee for the 1962 World Cup said: 'BECAUSE we do not have anything, we will do EVERYTHING to rebuild!' Understandably, this became the unofficial motto of the 1962 tournament staged in hurriedly reconstructed stadia and in a land still desperately ravaged by the disaster of two years before.

We too easily forget that the World Cup in England in 1966 was the second, not the first post-1945 tournament to be staged in defiance of almost unimaginable adversity.

Another thing which is neglected in the popular imagination is the fact that had England performed better in Chile in 1962 it might have stumbled into the 1966 World Cup with its traditional shackles still clanking as loudly as before.

The England squad which travelled to South America in May 1962 was managed by the redoubtable Walter Winterbottom but *selected* by the Football Association's eight-man 'selection committee'.

Initially, forty names were supplied to FIFA ahead of the deadline on 10th April, with eighteen men being disappointed when the final squad was announced on

15th April 1962. For reasons probably more likely to have been dictated by parsimony two of the 'final twenty-two' stayed behind in England as 'reserves', Gordon Banks, Leicester City's at that time uncapped goalkeeper, and West Bromwich Albion's Derek Kevan, a free-scoring striker who had scored two goals in the 1958 finals in Sweden. Just before the competition Banks was informed, he had been dropped so as to permit the inclusion of Bobby Moore, the twenty-one-year old West Ham United defender who had been included in the World Cup squad after impressing in his debut against Peru at Lima on 5th May. Kevan eventually travelled to Chile but was one of the nine men who never got onto the field.

In 1962 England had been drawn in a qualification group including Hungary, Argentina and Bulgaria, eventually reaching the quarter-final stage of the competition by coming second in the group by virtue of a superior goal average – goals scored divided by goals conceded – above Argentina.

England had stuttered and frustrated in the group matches; having had most of the play but losing against the Hungarians, outplaying Argentina and then being held to a goalless draw by the bottom team in the group, Bulgaria. In a tournament recognised in retrospect as being the first where the majority of the teams relied on organisation and tactical 'shape', and applied rigorous 'man to man', or 'zonal marking' systems, England were neither one thing nor the other.

These 'systems were mainly concerned with 'marking space' and thus, theoretically, denying it to the opposition. Obviously, it was more complicated than that but the author craves his reader's indulgence and plans to delve no deeper in the arcane intricacies or the mendacity of 'systems'; and hereafter, will attempt to pass a veil over much of that 'technical stuff' as possible! In any event it was not the 'systems' that were the problem, it was that the English game had also adopted that head in the sand attitude about modernity and foreign innovations.

Thus, Winterbottom's men could be well-organised, a team that passed and ran one day, or a boot it and hope outfit another but by 1962 there were times when native pluck and a profusion of honest sweat simply did not 'cut it' at the highest level any more.

In the Quarter-Final against the rampant Brazilians at Estadio Municipal, Viña del Mar, in Valparaíso on the 10th June 1962, Walter Winterbottom's brave boys held the Latin tide for forty-five minutes before, after valiant resistance going down to defeat by three goals to one. Garincha, Pelé and their fellow footballing invincibles were just too good for them and nobody was unduly surprised when Brazil went on – much in the manner of a regal procession – to lift the Jules Rimet Trophy for the second consecutive tournament a week or so later.

There was a deal of head scratching about how anybody, let alone England, could hope to compete with Brazil come 1966. Although Winterbottom's men had not exactly disgraced themselves; clearly if England was to mount a serious challenge four years hence then something had to change. And whatever it was, it needed to happen fairly soon!

Given that it was unlikely that the Football League was going to suddenly magic half-a-dozen once in a generation of geniuses out of a hat there was a recognition, a reluctant one, in the corridors of the Football Association that on the field at least, its representative teams ought to adopt 'modern' methods. Serendipitously, since 'their man', Walter Winterbottom had been wanting to move onto a less high profile, organisational and coaching role for some time, this gave room to bring in a man with a surfeit of contemporary club management experience.

Problematically, the obvious man – forty-two-year old Alfred 'Alf' Ernest Ramsey – the successful manager of Ipswich Town, was not entirely the Football Association's 'cup of tea'.

The Dagenham-born former wartime company quartermaster sergeant had never had anything to do with the university, public school and county 'chaps' who ran the FA and treated the governing body's 'sporting responsibilities' as essentially 'social' obligations. It is a moot question whether the FA Council would have worried over-much about England's middlingly disappointing performance in Chile, had the next World Cup not been in England, or that potentially, unless the national side bucked up its ideas Her Majesty the Queen might have to sit in the Royal Box in July 1966 watching two 'foreign' teams contest the next final.

Thus, it came to pass that insofar as the old boy's network which dominated the FA agreed about anything in 1962 it was that one way or another England had to put up a good show next time around and that the old ways – with amateur selection committees advising, meddling and often riding roughshod over the wishes of men like Walter Winterbottom, while positively deriding 'professionals' and 'professionalism' in the game – were going to have to be dispensed with.

If only because otherwise the FA was going to get blamed if it all ended in tears in 1966!

While it would be wrong to portray Winterbottom as a hidebound, backward thinking Football Association's stooge – he was anything but and should rightfully be seen as the invaluable transitional figure who, in effect, held the fort and to a degree, prepared the ground for what followed – it was obvious that by the early 1960s he was not the man to carry the national side forward.

By the summer of 1962 he had been the man in the firing line for one hundred and thirty-nine matches – of which the national side had won 78, drawn 33 and lost 28, scoring 383 goals and conceding 196 – over and sixteen long, and from time to time, thankless years.

Winterbottom had played for Manchester United prior to the Second War before ankylosing spondylitis had intervened, ending his playing days and he had resumed his career as a teacher. During the war he had worked at the Air Ministry – eventually becoming the Wing-Commander responsible for the training of RAF physical instructors worldwide – and once demobbed, the FA Council, at Sir Stanley Rous's prompting, had appointed him its first Director of Coaching. One gains a flavour of the mood of the time and the haphazard approach to these things that the role also included the job of *England Manager*.

Despite failing to make an impression – other than an abject impression more than once – in four World Cup Final tournaments, England only lost six home matches in Winterbottom's time 'in charge'. In that time England were usually British Champions – competing against Scotland, Wales and Northern Ireland, coming out on top thirteen times – and had never failed to actually qualify for the World Cup Finals.

It is a testimony to the underlying strength of the English game and Winterbottom's fortitude that he achieved what he did. It must have been thoroughly galling to never be allowed to pick his own team; condemned just to 'manage', to make the best of a bad deal with whomsoever the personnel his elders and betters thought best fitted – or simply 'liked the look of' – and yet to be the man held accountable for the performances of teams that were never truly 'his'. What modern manager would put up with a situation where a bunch of dilettantes picked 'his' eleven, took all the plaudits when they got it right and washed their hands of all responsibility when it went wrong?

Nevertheless, Winterbottom had put up with this increasingly intolerable situation over the years with unfailing good grace even though there must have been times when he wanted to tear his hair out!

In the end he had had enough.

His last act was to talk the FA Council into appointing a manager who henceforth would have complete control over selection; and it was the Chilean experience of June 1962 which finally convinced the FA that if they did not do something – and quickly – England was going to get left behind.

So, when Winterbottom resigned from the FA to take up the post of General Secretary of the CCPE – Central Council of Physical Education – in the autumn of 1962 the great men of the Football Association eventually, with what now seems stunningly uncharacteristic pragmatism turned to Alf Ramsey.

Ramsey had played over three hundred times for Southampton and Tottenham Hotspur, and thirty-two times for England as a combative, wily full back. As a player he had lacked a certain fleetness but had made up for it with a rare ability to 'read the game'.

Tellingly, even in his playing days his fellows had nicknamed Alf Ramsey 'the General'.

He had been a part of Tottenham's Championship winning side in 1951, captained his country three times and played for England in the 1950 World Cup, the tournament in which England has lost 1-0 to the amateur

United States side; the first but by no means the last of England's World Cup humiliations in the years to come.

Retiring from playing at the age of thirty-five he had gone into management, taking over struggling Ipswich Town, then languishing in the obscurity of the Third Division (South). Under Ramsey Ipswich had gained promotion to the Second Division and won promotion again as Champions of that division in the season of 1960-61. The next year Ipswich had won the Football League title. It had been at the end of the 1961-62 season that the Football Association had offered the brightest managerial star in the country the opportunity to mastermind England's campaign to win the World Cup of 1966.

On first acquaintance Ramsey could seem a cold fish, dour and introverted and his attempts to cast off his childhood accent – he was born in Dagenham in Essex – gave his voice a clipped, artificial precision that did not always ring true.

However, beneath his carefully maintained mask of cool detachment, he was one of the English game's genuine thinkers, he understood football and the men who played it, and above all he knew about 'winning'.

3 | Saturday 27th October 1962

Twenty-one-year old Geoffrey Charles Hurst's footballing career was at a crossroads that Saturday night as he took a copy of the *Evening Standard* from the boy vendor outside Chelmsford Railway Station. He had gone for a few drinks with friends from West Ham United's reserves after the match that afternoon at Upton Park – in front of a few hundred people – and heard that the first team had lost to Manchester United.

'The Hammers' nearby East End neighbours Leyton Orient had also lost, badly at home to Tottenham but 'the Orient' were on the way down and everybody knew it, so that had not caused anywhere near the comment that West Ham's three-one defeat at Old Trafford that afternoon had given rise to at the bar.

Yes, United had Bobby Charlton on the wing, that Scottish will-o'-the-wisp Denis Law in front of goal and that little Irish near-genius trickster Johnny Giles in the middle of the park but Matt Busby's team were no world-beaters. Goodness, they had been right at the foot of the table before the match, even now they would only be one point off the bottom; while the Hammers had been in the top half – in tenth position – at the start of the day!

Geoff Hurst ran his eye down that afternoon's League Division One scores.

Arsenal 5-4 Wolverhampton Wanderers
Birmingham 3-2 Aston Villa
Bolton Wanderers 1-0 Nottingham Forest
Burnley 0-0 Manchester City
Everton 3-1 Ipswich Town
Fulham 0-0 Blackburn Rovers
Leicester City 3-1 Sheffield United
Leyton Orient 1-5 Tottenham Hotspur
Manchester United 3-1 West Ham United
Sheffield Wednesday 0-0 Blackpool
West Bromwich Albion 1-0 Liverpool

Burnley had been at the top of the pile that morning but both Tottenham and Everton would have leapfrogged them this afternoon.

There was a scruffy, abbreviated report of the Old Trafford game inside the back page. Albert Quixall, one of United's first big signings after the Munich air disaster back in 1958 – for the then princely sum of £45,000 from Sheffield Wednesday – had scored two goals and Denis Law the other, with Malcolm Musgrove, who had recently become the Chairman of the Professional Footballers' Association notching a consolation goal in return.

Arsenal and Wolves must have had a rare old ding-dong of it at Highbury but there were few other surprises.

At training yesterday morning, the boys had been optimistic about taking on United when the Old Trafford men had been going through a 'quiet patch'; but you could never quite tell *which* United you were going to come up against on the day.

Pos.	Team	P.	W.	D.	L.	For	Ag.	PTS.
1	Tottenham Hotspur	15	10	2	3	54	26	22
2	Everton	14	10	2	2	31	15	22
3	Burnley	15	8	5	2	32	23	21
4	Leicester City	15	8	4	3	31	18	20
5	Wolverhampton W.	15	8	3	4	35	25	19
6	Aston Villa	15	8	2	5	28	24	18
7	Nottingham Forest	14	7	3	4	28	24	17
8	Sheff. Wednesday	15	6	5	4	28	26	17
9	Sheff. United	15	6	4	5	25	25	16
10	West Bromwich A.	15	6	3	6	26	25	15
11	Blackpool	15	4	6	5	17	22	14
12	West Ham United	15	4	5	6	26	26	13
13	Blackburn Rovers	15	5	3	7	23	29	13
14	Manchester City	15	4	5	6	21	36	13
15	Arsenal	14	4	4	6	25	29	12
16	Bolton Wanderers	15	5	2	8	22	27	12
17	Birmingham City	15	4	4	7	20	31	12

18	Liverpool	14	4	3	7	18	21	11
19	Ipswich Town	15	2	6	7	22	26	10
20	Manchester United	15	4	2	9	22	32	10
21	Fulham	15	3	4	8	14	27	10
22	Leyton Orient	15	4	1	10	17	28	9

The young footballer had nursed his drinks, drunk only a pint-and-a-half while several of his mates had got legless; which was probably why so many of them were still in the reserves.

Hurst had missed out today because twenty-five-year old Johnny 'Budgie' Byrne and Peter Braybrook, both England internationals had got the nod up front ahead of him. West Ham had paid a record £65,000 to Crystal Palace for Budgie – he talked all the time – to bring him to Upton Park that spring; and Pete Braybrook had played for England in the 1958 World Cup in Sweden against the USSR.

Geoff Hurst's manager, Ron Greenwood, who had arrived at West Ham in April 1961, had decided that he lacked what it took to be a left-sided defensive midfielder and at any rate, Bobby Moore who had played for England in that summer's World Cup in Chile – with whom he had come through the ranks since signing apprentice terms at the age of fifteen – pretty much owned that place in the team. The 'boss' wanted Hurst to play up front but thus far opportunities had been limited – Budgie Byrne owned the number nine shirt and Braybrook was not about to give up his number ten slot without a fight – so most of the time the young professional was trying to keep his spirits up scoring goals for the reserves.

He had been dropped after the first match of the season on grounds of 'not being match fit'. Ron Greenwood had been distinctly unimpressed with him on his return from playing cricket with Essex that summer; and presently, Hurst was beginning to wonder when – or if - he would ever get a decent run in the first team.

Geoff Hurst was a wartime baby, born in December 1941 in Ashton-under-Lyne, a long way away from the East London and Essex roots of most of his apprentice contemporaries when he joined the club in 1956. His family had moved to Chelmsford when he was six and from a very young age, he had always been a natural all-round sportsman. That had never been a problem until now; but Ron Greenwood had made it clear they did not need a cricketer-footballer who was 'quite good' at both sports – he had been dismissed twice without scoring in his only first-class, top level outing with Essex County Cricket Club – 'the boss' wanted a man dedicated to West Ham United and to honing the fitness and skills required of a full-time professional footballer.

Hurst's father, Charlie, had played professionally for Bristol Rovers, Oldham and Rochdale, and Geoff had hugely enjoyed turning out for Essex seconds as a wicketkeeper who could bat more than tolerably well. Thus far he had been able to combine his two sporting loves but that autumn it was as if he had just hit a brick wall.

His youthful resilience, strength and physicality had convinced Ron Greenwood's predecessor, Ted Fenton to offer him professional terms in 1958. In those days £7 per week and a whopping great big £20 signing on fee had seemed like a fortune! However, it was about then that he realised that Bobby Moore was twice the player he was in his chosen position; no matter, he had a second cricketing string to his bow.

All that had changed with the arrival of Ron Greenwood: forget about the kick and run football of the past, he expected his men to get the ball on the ground, to feet, and to pass; and to develop and demonstrate pure footballing skills.

At the start of the season the prospect of a partnership 'up front' with the chatty, mercurial Budgie Byrne had beckoned, now he was in and out of the team and a less strong-minded young man might have wondered if he had missed the boat.

In the meantime, all he could do was train hard, do his level best in the reserves and every time he got a chance to run out in a big match to seize the day.

Asked in later years if on that evening he had ever dreamed of playing for England, or of participating in the far away World Cup still nearly four years down the road Geoff Hurst was always coy.

'Every kid dreams of playing for England, obviously...'

As for the World Cup?

'No, I don't think I ever thought about that. Getting into the West Ham team was what I lived and slept. I didn't think I was half the player that Budgie Byrne was; Ron Greenwood used to compare Budgie with Alfredo Di Stéfano, and I was surrounded by people like Bobby Moore, and Martin Peters... Martin was the classiest of the lot, but who remembers him now, more's the pity?'

Like many of the survivors of that night in late October 1962 Geoff Hurst often spoke as if the war had torn the heart out of a golden generation of players. The 'golden generation' who might have been in its prime in the summer of 1966. He was a young man aware that he was living in a time of change and that the future belonged to him, to his 'generation' and that the times were changing.

Only a year before professional footballers in England had broken the shackles of the £20 a week cap on their wages; already by the season of 1962-63 stars like Fulham's Johnny Haynes were earning over £5000 *a year*! These were unheard of riches to a generation of young sportsmen no longer threatened by the blight of National Service, which had interrupted so many brilliant careers in the 1950s, now living in a society where all the old norms and restrictions now seemed if not threatened, then at least, no longer immutable.

Geoff Hurst knew that he was on the cusp of a career his parents could only have dreamed of. It might not include the honour of representing his country but playing for West Ham United, one of the more 'upwardly mobile' clubs in the land managed by a man who looked to the future not the past for his inspiration, was by no means a poor second. Injury or failing to come up to scratch might yet wreck his career; that was the way of things. But either way, success or failure was in his hands, or rather, at his feet.

And then at around three o'clock on the morning of Sunday 28th October 1962 a thermonuclear warhead estimated to be in the 1.5 to 1.7 megaton range initiated high in the sky above Brentwood some thirteen-and-a-half miles from Geoff Hurst's digs in Essex and blew asunder the life that he had hoped and planned to live.

When Geoff Hurst regained consciousness

approximately six hours later, he was briefly trapped beneath rubble a floor below where he had been asleep. Miraculously, he had escaped serious injury – other than for a concussion, and probably a hairline fracture of the skull – bar three cracked ribs because the mattress on which he had been asleep had fallen with him from the first-floor bedroom, breaking his fall as the outer wall of the house was ripped away by the blast over-pressure wave of the largest of the Soviet bombs to explode over the Greater London Area.

4 | The Ghost of FIFA

The World might have half blown itself up in late October 1962 but politics never really goes away. Especially, in sport.

Bizarrely, soon after the war there were people in France and in Switzerland who still believed that they were 'FIFA'. In a surreal dance around reality in the 'through the looking glass' world of footballing international bureaucracy, not least by men staffing UEFA's Swiss headquarters in un-bombed Geneva – yes, they were all men – who still thought that in the post-apocalyptic era that their organisations should carry on 'as normal'. But then let it not be forgotten that there was a deal of 'headless chicken' activity in England as the Football Association sought to lobby members of the 1963 UKIEA (United Kingdom Interim Emergency Administration, 28th October 1962 to 31st December 1963), and the 1964 UAUK (Unity Administration of the United Kingdom, 1st January 1964 to 9th March 1965) governments to facilitate the re-starting of the professional game when plainly, the country was barely managing to feed itself and the authorities were horrified by the very idea of having to 'steward' and 'defend' regular large gatherings.

That a reduced, semi-professional Football League competition – essentially a cut down version of its pre-war incarnation – was played out in the season of 1963-64 in England, and that four eighteen to twenty team leagues were again in operation, and the FA Cup re-launched in 1964-65, albeit in a somewhat ad hoc, chaotic fashion with minimal Government help was both a compliment to, and a demonstration of the stubbornness and arrogance of the owners of the surviving clubs and the Football Association which was to sour relations with regional and national authorities for years to come.

While it might seem obvious to our modern sensibilities that the staging of large sporting events ought not to have been allowed to be resumed other than in areas where the pre-war infrastructure was still largely intact, or where the rule of law had been firmly re-entrenched; that was not the accepted wisdom of the times.

The modern legal requirement for the 'parties organising public events to be responsible for the safety and the costs caused to the public purse from the same' stem in the main from the blunders of the mid to late 1960s and the numerous public order disasters, and not to put too fine a point on it 'riots' which blighted many large cities almost entirely because of the cavalier, profiteering methods of the club owners which the Football league, and the Football Association did little or nothing to mitigate until legislation eventually imposed severe, and very personal penalties, on the directors of clubs and tournament organisers.

Many social historians associate the political fallout from the Bramall Lane Disaster, in which ultimately it was estimated that over a hundred and forty people attending a Labour Party election rally in March 1965 were killed and hundreds injured with later 'public event' legislation but Cabinet records show that Members of Mrs Thatcher's first administration were mainly preoccupied with 'Association Football' matches.

But that is to digress. The subject of the way British society and the organisation of football developed and was regulated more properly belongs to a book about the latter 1960s and England's World Cup campaign of 1970!

By early 1964 the rump of FIFA had re-established itself in Rome, where for reasons best known to itself the Fascist regime took its presence as a mark of its self-importance and made available the communications facilities of the Italian state, such as survived in the chaos of those times, for the 'football men' to spread their message.

This greatly offended Sir Stanley Rous, the incumbent President of FIFA whom the 'administrators' in Rome's FIFA secretariat did not or were not permitted to 'recognise' presumably on the basis that he was an Englishman and Romano-United Kingdom relations were at their lowest ebb since 1943. Much though the Italian government wanted to write off the Regia Aeronautica's sneak attack on Malta in December 1963 as an 'unfortunate error' the British side were having none of it.

Over the years FIFA had done a lot of things to upset

the FA and the British Government and memories were long. The fact that the 'office' of the Fédération Internationale de Football Association had 're-opened for business' in the capital of what was considered an 'unfriendly power' simply exacerbated the sting of all the already wounded feelings in England.

Back in 1960 many in the England camp had been touchy about the subject of Spain having possibly dropped out of the bidding contest to assist 'the Germans'. At this remove we forget that the Second War was still fresh in the minds of most of the participants and although West Germany was by then a good NATO ally, Spain's less than honourable neutrality between 1939 and 1945 was one of many points of friction with the regime of the Generalissimo in Madrid.

Had it been widely known at the time that between 1940 and 1945 the British Government had had to bribe General Franco and his coterie to stay out of the Second World War, depositing much scarce treasure in numbered Swiss bank accounts, any hint of Iberian collusion with the Germans in 1960 would have given the British press a positive field day! In any event the whole affair had 'tickled' a lot of half-buried sensitivities that nobody really wanted to ventilate back in 1960, and even the FA – with its traditionally Elephantine-thick skin – was mindful that the last thing it wanted, or needed, to do was salt old wounds when it belatedly remembered that IT had been awarded the right to host the World Cup of 1966!

History as they say 'never really goes away'.

It was a moot point if, in the spring of 1964 when Sir Stanley Rous, John 'Joe' Mears – the Chairman of the Football Association – and Sir Harold Warris Thompson, the University don and scientist who was actually the man behind the throne at the post-October War FA, were actually as convinced as they later claimed that there was any real legitimacy to the claim that the World Cup of 1966 was still England's to host.

However, what the three men knew for an absolute certainty was that with the European hegemony over FIFA – or for any successor World governing body – permanently shattered by the recent war if there was another vote, the South and Central American block led by Brazil, Argentina, Uruguay and Mexico would either delay, reschedule or 'purloin' the next tournament for themselves!

This is in fact, exactly what happened with Mexico (1970), Brazil (1974) and Argentina (1978) 'earning' the right to host all three World Cup tournaments in the 1970s.

Paranoia aside, the FA could hardly claim to have been the most loyal or obedient of FIFA's members down the years; which was why many countries felt it 'went against the grain' giving England the World Cup in 1966 in the first place. At such times people recollected how often in the past the FA had sanctimoniously seized the moral high ground to the detriment of its 'imperial' and 'foreign' opponents almost always citing the 'sanctity of sport' in the name of supposedly 'Olympian values'.

In 1905 the FA and the other 'British Associations' – at the time the Welsh, Scottish and Irish – were latecomers to FIFA; and had walked out in 1914 when the organisation failed to expel their Great War Central Power enemies (Germany, Austria, et al) and not come back into the fold until 1924. The FA's return had been short-lived, falling out with FIFA over the Olympian definition of 'amateurism' and so-called 'broken-time payments' to otherwise unpaid, non-professional athletes including footballers. England had not therefore, played in the inaugural World Cup of 1930 in Uruguay, or the competitions of 1934 or 1938. Then, when the FA had finally returned to FIFA's ranks in 1946 its first initiative had been to demand that the German and Japanese Associations be thrown out.

While both Germany and Japan were re-admitted to FIFA in 1950 having been denied the opportunity to qualify for the 1950 Finals; coincidentally, England's first and somewhat ill-starred introduction to the tournament.

Evidently, it came as a big surprise when the letter from England arrived in Rome in February 1965 informing the Acting Secretary of FIFA that the President, Sir Stanley Rous proposed that the World Cup Finals of 1966 go ahead as planned.

It took a month for FIFA's response to reach England.

'The Board of the Fédération Internationale de Football Association has determined to defer the

tournament for two years so that an extraordinary Congress can be called to decide on the future development of the World game...'

The main objection of the Roman secretariat of FIFA was that there was no time in which to organise qualification matches for the 1966 tournament.

Moreover, due to the exigencies of the 'recent war' no contracts between FIFA and the Football Association had been discussed – this was a new twist, the first time the governing body had, mafia-like, demanded its cut of the gate receipts – and nobody in Rome believed it was remotely 'safe' to play international soccer in England.

The texts of the communications emanating from Rome in those days now read like something out of a Ruritanian farce which is explicable only in the context of 'the Board of FIFA' being completely in the pocket of the regime in Rome which, realising the English had stolen a march on them, had concluded it would be a good idea to stage the World Cup of 1966 themselves. Specifically, in Rome, Naples and Florence!

Sir Stanley Rous soon put a stop to this nonsense:

'The Board of the Fédération Internationale de Football Association cannot have 'sat' since I, as President was not forewarned of its sitting and had I, been so informed, I would have dismissed it. The decision of 22nd June 1960 stands: England will host the World Cup of 1966 and given the exigencies of the World situation the sixteen teams who will compete in the tournament will be those nominated by the South American Football Confederation (CONMEBOL, the Confederación Sudamericana de Fútbol), and Confederation of North, Central American and Caribbean Association Football (CONCACAF) up to a maximum of six national teams. In addition to the English team Scotland, Northern Ireland and Wales will be invited to participate. Five other teams from Europe will be included in the draw (these to be nominated by UEFA in consultation with FIFA). In the interests of the broader World game a country from Africa will be invited (this

nation to be selected by the Confederation of African Football).'

In the event that UEFA and or FIFA failed to provide a qualification and or nomination list of non-British teams to contest the World Cup by 31st December 1965 the Football Association reserved the right to issue its own invitations compete in the tournament.

Rous concluded by informing the 'Roman FIFA' that the 1966 tournament would conform to the model of the previous World Cup in Chile in 1962. The sixteen teams would be divided into four 'qualifying groups', with each team playing three round-robin matches to decide the eight quarter-finalists. The quarter-finals would be contested by the top two teams in each qualifying group. The winning quarter-finalists would contest semi-finals, and the winners of those matches would go forward to the final. The losing semi-finalists would play in the 'third place match' two days before the final, provisionally scheduled for Saturday 23th July 1966.

Oh, and the Football Association would not be paying any 'fees, miscellaneous out of course disbursements, or agency costs to FIFA in respect of the tournament'.

5 | Can We Actually Do This?

The World Cup of 1966 only happened because, according to Edward Ralph "Ted" Dexter, MP, Minister for Sport and Recreation 1965-67: 'We were given the right to hold it in Rome in 1960; two-and-half great men of English football decided as much, and Argentina!'

I have said enough about Rome 1960 so herein let us concentrate on the second and third clauses of this statement.

The two-and-a-half great men of English football were Sir Stanley Rous, John 'Joe' Mears, and Harold Warris Thompson; and Ted Dexter was destined to regale countless appreciative audiences on the 'wining, dining and public speaking circuit' with entertaining accounts of his first, in retrospect momentous meeting, with the 'FA Three'.

The encounter had taken place at Dexter's office at the Ministry of Sport – a hastily prefabricated structure in the Parks at Oxford - a couple of months after the first post-war General Election in March 1965.

Fortunately, there is a more definitive record of the meeting, courtesy of the contemporaneous notes taken by Dexter's Permanent Secretary, Robin Butler and it is his notes rather than his Minister's later recollections that this author bases what follows.

The then seventy-two-year-old Sir Stanley Rous was the grand old man of World football, a thing acknowledged by his election as President of FIFA in London in 1961.

Butler remembers that John 'Joe' Mears looked 'like he was going to drop dead on his feet at any moment'. Mears had been the Chairman of Chelsea Football Club, which no longer existed other than in the dreams of its few surviving patrons and fans, and of the English Football Association at the time of the October War. That day Mears's only preoccupation was finding a chair to sit on before he fell over, hence Dexter's possibly unjust initial opinion – one he was to radically revise in the coming months - that he was the 'half-man' of the trio. Ironically, most people now credit Mears for doing much of the 'legwork' and 'arm-twisting' which enabled the tournament to actually 'get off the ground' up and down the country.

Fifty-seven-year-old Harold Warris Thompson was a renowned physical chemist who had taught Margaret Thatcher at Oxford in the early 1950s. Although officially only a 'mere member' of the Committee of the FA he had walked into Dexter's office like he owned it, smoking a cigar.

Robin Butler had done his homework on the three 'footballing men' and fully briefed his Minister. Still only twenty-seven he was already a high-flyer in the war-winnowed Home Civil Service posted to Dexter's department basically to hold his new minister's hand until 'he got the hang of things'. Actually, the two men – Dexter was only thirty months Butler's senior – got on like a house on fire and became lifelong friends.

Sir Stanley Rous, a man of Suffolk, had trained to be a teacher before the First War, during which he had served in the ranks as an artilleryman in France and the Levant. Completing his teacher training after that war he had taught at Watford Boys Grammar School; in his playing days he was a goalkeeper in the amateur game before his career was cut short by injury, thereafter he had become a referee, overseeing his first international match – between Belgium and the Netherlands – in 1927 and taking charge of the FA Cup Final between Manchester City and Portsmouth in 1934.

Rous was the man who had re-written the Laws of Football in 1938 and was the instigator of the 'diagonal system of control' – where a referee did not attempt to slavishly follow the ball but ran 'diagonal lines' across the field so as to always have the best, and widest view of play. His long career as an international referee had only ended the year before the October War, when he was sixty-five on his being voted 6th President of the Fédération Internationale de Football Association.

Rous might not have made his name as a player but as a referee and administrator he was indubitably the 'great man' of the game; and that day his bearing broadcast the fact loud and clear. He was clearly a man on a mission and that was a thing that Robin Butler's new minister, a quick learner, had realised was always a very bad sign in political life.

John 'Joe' Mears, the Chairman of the Football Association was another former amateur goalkeeper. He was the son of Joseph Mears, the co-founder of Chelsea Football Club. His uncle, Gus, was the club's other founding father. Becoming a director of that club in 1931 at the age of twenty-six, he had been its chairman since 1940. During the Second War he had been an officer in the Royal Marines, and at one time responsible for safeguarding the bunkers housing the wartime Government in London. Before the recent war the Mears family had owned not only Chelsea Football Club but a chain of cinemas.

Mears was the man who had over-ruled everybody else at Chelsea to bring the then Reading manager Ted Drake, the former Southampton and Arsenal striker, to Stamford Bridge – the now wrecked former home of his club – in 1952, a decision vindicated within two years by the club winning the Division 1 Championship. Less in his favour was that he had been one of the eight – yes eight - members of the England selection panel which selected the sides that lost 7-1 in Budapest, and 6-3 to the Hungarians at Wembley in the 1950s, and singularly failed to persuade his colleagues in Europe of the merits of staging a European International Championship in the early 1950s, an idea that was, it seemed, rather too ahead of its time in that now lost era.

If Rous was the greying, blustering footballing figurehead of the triumvirate then Mears was the hard-headed business man, the man who actually got his hands dirty and got things done. However, right from the outset both Dexter and Butler decided that the man really calling the shots was Harold Thompson.

Thompson was a Yorkshireman, born the son of a colliery manager at Wombwell. Educated at King Edward VII School in Sheffield, and Trinity College, Oxford; where he had been tutored by Sir Cyril Hinshelwood, who had been awarded the Nobel Prize for Chemistry in 1956. Later Thompson had worked with Fritz Haber and Max Planck at the Friedrich Wilhelm University in Berlin, which was where he had received his Ph.D. During the Second War he had worked in the field of infra-red spectroscopy for the Ministry of Aircraft Production, afterwards he become a Fellow of the Royal Society and

Vice President of St John's College, Oxford, which was where in the early 1950s he had taught the Prime Minister, herself a chemist.

As a young man Thompson had won a blue at football at Oxford, and ever after been passionately involved with the Oxford University Association Football Club. He was one of the movers behind establishing the annual Varsity Match at Wembley with Cambridge, and he set up the Pegasus Club in 1948; the club of former Oxford and Cambridge University players which in the 1950s had twice won the FA Amateur Cup: beating Bishop Auckland 2-1 in 1951, and Harwich and Parkeston 6-0 in 1953 in front of capacity 100.000 crowds at Wembley. By May 1965 had established himself as a decidedly over-mighty member of the Football Association's Council. *After* 1966 Thompson was to become the virtual 'dictator' of English football. Some thought this a good thing, others not. His reputation was best summed up by a former FA official '...he was a bullying autocrat. He was a bastard. He treated the staff like shit.'

Thompson was one of those men sometimes respected and admired but who was not generally liked. For all that he was known to be an inspiring teacher he was only happy when he was calling the shots.

Ted Dexter recognised what he was up against.

The great man had removed his cigar from his mouth as he and the Minister for Sport shook hands; then he had frowned as he looked around for an ash tray.

'I don't encourage smoking in my rooms, sir,' Dexter informed him apologetically. 'Robin, if you could find something for Mr Thompson to extinguish his cigar in, please?'

The other thing about Harold Thompson was that he never forgot, or forgave an offence once given.

'I just knew the fellow was going to try to blow smoke – metaphorically at least – in my face," Dexter would guffaw in later years. 'Thompson gave me the sort of schoolmasterish look I'd been used to getting from certain antediluvian members of the MCC Committee before the October War!'

Dexter had ignored *that* look; knowing that today he was the one with the whip hand.

'Well, gentlemen,' he had smiled as chairs scraped

and the five men in the office took their places. 'The floor is yours; how can I help you?'

'You may not be aware, Mr Dexter,' Sir Stanley Rous had prefaced without looking at either of his lieutenants, 'that back on the 22nd June 1960 in Rome the Football Association defeated the West Germans by thirty-four votes to twenty-seven, the Spanish having dropped out of the competition, to win the right to host the Fédération Internationale de Football Association World Cup in 1966.'

Actually, the Minister of Sport did recollect that there had been somewhat muted comment on this subject in the sporting pages of the papers before the war. Most of the coverage had been ribald, a little dismissive subsequent to the England team's mediocre showing in the World Cup of 1962 held in Chile. He had not given the matter another thought.

'I assumed that had all been overtaken by events?' He had queried, his interest piqued.

'No,' Rous retorted. 'FIFA exists 'in being' in Rome; although not actively at the present time but its past rulings and decisions still govern the international game. I still consider myself to be its Chairman and I will remain so until such time as a properly convened meeting and election confirms or unseats me. I therefore, speak for the game internationally, in the same way that Mr Mears and Professor Thompson speak for it in England.'

At this juncture Ted Dexter had glanced involuntarily at Robin Butler, who shrugged imperceptibly.

Harold Thompson had sighed impatiently.

'Just tell him, Stanley,' he had grunted impatiently.

Sir Stanley Rous took a moment to collect his thoughts.

'We plan to stage the tournament as planned next summer!'

Without Ted Dexter's explicit support this thing would go no further than Rous's defiant statement of intent. Even with the former England Cricket Captain's imprimatur any one of half-a-dozen ministries could veto the whole project in the blink of an eye. In fact, 'the tournament' was the sort of thing that would only happen if it had the active backing of a member of the Prime Minister's inner circle. Or perhaps, of the Prime Minister herself.

'The Home Office is bound to point to the difficulties large sporting events might cause in the field of public good order,' he suggested. 'Then how on earth do you propose to transport large numbers of people to matches?' He hated to be a killjoy but: 'Is it financially viable to stage such a tournament in the present economic climate?'

Joe Mears had stirred; in this group he was the businessman with the practical, hands on experience of making things happen and making a profit out of it.

'The professional game in England is bankrupt,' he observed. 'Inflation being what it is, well, for anything that's not rationed, that is, most people can't even afford a few coppers to go through the turnstiles to watch a football match...'

This apparently defeatist attitude obviously displeased Harold Thompson.

'Just because we don't like the odds that's no reason to give in, Joe,' he had declared gruffly. 'What would have happened last year at Malta or in the Persian Gulf if our brave boys had thrown in the towel the moment the going got tough? Our players wear the three lions' badge on their chests; we never surrender!'

'Surely,' Ted Dexter interjected, 'the original plans would have included employing the Empire Stadium at Wembley to host some of the bigger matches?'

'Yes,' Thompson shot back.

'Well,' Dexter went on, 'that won't be possible...'

'Why not?' The older man had snapped dismissively. 'The roof's gone, there's a lot of rubble on the pitch but the fabric of the stadium is still in more or less one piece. The Royal Engineers already have a big depot at Wembley Park. I took a couple of structural engineers down to Wembley last week to look around. There are a couple of railway lines nearby, neither of them that badly damaged all things considered, and if somebody got their fingers out the roads around it could be cleared. In East London the Army's set up their headquarters at what's left of West Ham's ground. Yes, the Upton Park stadium wasn't as close to a really big bomb as Wembley but they're both still standing. There's a lot of talk in this city about the priorities for reconstruction, quite apart from all that nonsense about creating a 'London Garden City'; well, we're giving you a reason to actually do something 'concrete' to 'kick off' the rebuilding of our capital city. Unless you can think of something better, staging the World Cup in this country next year is as good a way to start as any!'

Fighting talk was one thing...

'That's a good argument, I'll grant that,' Dexter had conceded, his thoughts turning over the problems and the – undeniably exciting - possibilities of the proposition. 'But it is an argument that, in one form or another, is being advanced by countless interested parties and lobby groups all over the country.'

Since the election Oxford had been crowded with flimflam men – and women – bidding, pleading, imploring the new Government to prioritise this or that unrealistic, over-ambitious or just plain hair-brained scheme. The whole nation had been fired up; everything seemed possible again.

The problem was that the country was still just as insolvent the day after the election as it had been the day before. True, the days of coalition and short-term political uncertainty were over and consequently the United Kingdom's bargaining – or 'begging' – voice vis-a-vis the United States was immeasurably stronger but the notional longer-term benefits this might accrue were no help to man or beast right now.

'I thought you liked a gamble, Mr Dexter?' Harold Thompson had asked abruptly, directly challenging the younger man.

'Now and then,' the former England Cricket captain nodded. 'But not blind punts; which is what you seem to be advocating.'

'Fair enough,' the older man guffawed. He had told the others that this would be a waste of time if they did not 'play for keeps'. He looked to Sir Stanley Rous. 'Do you want to tell him or shall I?'

Ted Dexter had recognised that the dynamic of the meeting had altered, switched to a higher intensity.

Sir Stanley Rous groaned but nodded his assent.

'If we fail to exercise our right to stage the World Cup by the end of next summer, then somebody else will, Minister,' he said ponderously.

The Minister for Sport did not immediately see the problem.

'Well, the game must go on,' he half-smiled.

'If somebody else runs with the ball,' Rous countered, his tone that of an old man putting down a disrespectful schoolboy. 'It may be Brazil, but more likely it will be the Argentines who will host the World Cup in the autumn of 1966!'

We were given the right to hold it in Rome in 1960; two-and-half great men of English football decided as much, and Argentina!

Until the previous July the United Kingdom had been at war with the Argentine. The Argentines had invaded and ejected the population of the Falkland Archipelago (over which *they* had a nominal territorial claim), seized South Georgia and the South Sandwich Islands (over which *they* had no claim whatsoever), murdering, torturing and heinously mistreating captured British servicemen and civilians alike in the process. In retaliation the Royal Navy had instituted a submarine blockade of the Falklands Archipelago and large areas of the South Atlantic, sinking several ships of the *Armada de la República Argentina*, including the aircraft carrier *Indepencia* with heavy loss of life.

In May 1965 an uneasy – and undeclared or acknowledged – ceasefire existed in the South Atlantic and it was tacitly, if not yet explicitly, accepted within Government circles, and no less in the population at large, that the country had unfinished business down in the South Atlantic. Thus, the very idea that the Argentine – the nation of the reviled despoilers of Port Stanley and of the killers, torturers and rapists who had preyed on the exiled, dispossessed people of the Falklands – should be permitted to steal *England's World Cup* was like waving a red rag at a bull.

The Government could just about stomach the tournament being lost to Brazil, or even some other 'civilised' Latin American country but ARGENTINA...

6 | Over My Dead Body!

Politics, politics, politics... Anybody who says that the World Cup of 1966 was *just* a football tournament – was in the words of one famous commentator – 'not paying attention!'

The roll of honour listing those whose commitment and work made it possible to host the World Cup in England in 1966 must include, right at the top John 'Joe' Mears, the Chairman of the Football Association; Minister of Sport and Recreation, former England Cricket Captain Edward 'Ted' Dexter; the Minister for London, Miriam Prior; Brigadier, later Lieutenant General David Willison, RE, the then Chief Surveyor of London, and a host of others but the whole enterprise could not possibly have got off the ground without the whole-hearted support of the United Kingdom Government, and in particular the unswerving backing of the Prime Minister. In an environment in which the allocation of scarce national resources had until – the summer of 1965 - literally been a matter of life and death, had Margaret Thatcher not unambiguously put her imprimatur on the project it simply would not, nor could it ever, have happened.

Afterwards, the 'Argentina factor' is often cited as being the beginning and the end of any discussion about the lady's infamous 'over my dead body' remark when informed that if England stepped aside then Argentina would probably hold the tournament. However, that ignores an underlying narrative. At the time the decision was taken to hold the competition in England, notwithstanding Margaret Thatcher's National Conservative Government – then recently elected with a landslide majority – was still in its post-victory 'honeymoon' period the scale of the problems confronting it were becoming ever more horribly stark.

Across the English Channel what was left of Western Europe was wrecked or in turmoil, or both. The 'French situation' remained unresolved, farther abroad there were intractable short-, medium- and long-term dilemmas everywhere, and at home it would be several years before 'food security' ceased to be the Government's number one priority. The country was in a mess, one-third smashed and now that the immediate crises of the post-October War period seemed to be behind the nation nobody really knew where to start the multi-generational task of reconstruction.

Today we look back and laud visionary's like Miriam Prior and a veritable pantheon of other 'heroes of the reconstruction' but in 1965 re-building was still no more than a pipedream and frankly, the task seemed insurmountable.

However, if things had begun to 'settle down' then all that really meant in practice was that people at last had time to worry about the raised post-war background radiation level, they were less patient with their hunger, intolerant of the shortage of antibiotics and the general dilapidation of the surviving health services, housing stocks and the scarcity of the thousand and one other things a modern society needs for its ongoing happy sustenance.

Margaret Thatcher, as her papers from the time reveal, was preoccupied from the moment she became Prime Minister in December 1963 with thoughts of great, unifying projects; endeavours in which everybody could invest, take pride in and in their hearts and minds, own. Those 'projects' could not be wars, they might be technological marvels, or more prosaically simply be to do with steadily, incrementally, remorselessly improving the lot of the man and the woman on the street. She believed that education had to be a big part of it; obviously, putting roofs over people's heads, calories in their stomachs; and moreover, the people needed to be, and ought to be proud of what they had achieved.

None of the things government did could be in isolation; we fight to defend ourselves and our allies, in return we trade, support, succour our friends and they do likewise to us. When we build it is for the good of all not the privileged few; similarly, 'the ration' is the ration for 'us all' without exception. There were no fat men – or women – in her administration, those people stayed on her back benches. We are all in this together or we are nothing!

The message got twisted, confused and diluted from time to time but its core still rings out loud and clear down the years. Oddly, in the summer of 1965 the fact that the idea of staging the Football World Cup of 1966 a year later was self-evidently absurd was in many ways, probably its biggest attraction to Margaret Thatcher.

In her calculus the 'ARGENTINA or US proposition' was the clinching; but not the winning, fundamental argument. So much is lost in translation even looking at events only two generations ago. Often it is nigh impossible to establish what happened; let alone why it happened.

Margaret Thatcher's 'OVER MY DEAD BODY!' assertion to Ted Dexter was and remains marvellous knockabout *copy*, ultimately, this author leaves it to the reader to decide where it ought to rank for the sake of posterity. In any event, in respect of so many of the events of that long ago, never to be forgotten summer of 1966 – a year scarred by the tragedy of wars fought, mercifully far from England's fair shore – the apocryphal has since become legend, indelibly ingrained on the British psyche.

Although afterwards a lot of people – and factions – forgot how vehemently they had cried foul about the waste of valuable resources 'just for a few games of football' in 1965 and the first half of 1966, folk memory generally holds that everybody in England jumped a veritable jig of joy when the Minister of Sport sat down with the 'FA Three' – Rous, Mears and Thompson – in July 1966 to formally announce to the nation's gathered press that the Government had decided to throw its 'whole weight and prestige' behind the enterprise.

In fact, the Labour Party – insofar as that Party had a single voice in those days - was dead set against it; and so were as many as sixty Conservative Members of Parliament who went so far as to sign an early day motion in the House of Commons in January 1966 to the effect that it was not too late to call the whole misbegotten 'circus' off. Then there were vociferous calls to ban the Argentine team, and subsequently, the Italians and a huge row – several, actually - broke out over why exactly, none of the matches were being played in Scotland or Wales or Northern Ireland with MPs and self-appointed 'community leaders' popping out of the woodwork to have their say, mainly to vent their bile, virtually until the first ball was kicked in July.

The mood of the three 'other' Home Football Associations was hardly soothed when, by then exasperated and 'sick to the back teeth' of the 'endless bickering' which 'must make the Government think we are all idiots', John Joe Mears had asked, somewhat plaintively, 'which part of ENGLAND WERE AWARDED THE 1966 FINALS DO YOU NOT UNDERSTAND?' His question being directed at a director of the Glasgow Rangers club.

A more mundane matter was what happened if visiting teams refused to live 'on the ration', and if they refused how on earth could England, or the other home country elevens could possibly compete on a 'level playing field'. When it became known that under one of the exceptional clauses of the War Emergency Acts the Minister of Sport had allocated 'ration uplifts' for the players of all four Home countries short-listed in April 1966 to 'level that playing field', there was an outcry in the national press and the Football Association and individual players began to get hate mail. This, like other furores subsided eventually, mainly because at around that time professional sports men – there were no professional sports *women* in the United Kingdom in that era - were re-classified as 'manual workers – heavy duties' and therefore entitled to up to double the national adult male daily ration under the increasingly relaxed regime of the spring of 1966.

The rationing of so-called food 'staples' came to an end in the United Kingdom on 1st June 1966. Some 'luxury items' remained 'on the ration' for another year; and as late as 1974 the Government retained Draconian powers to 'manage the allocation of food and medicines and other essential supplies in times of seasonal or exceptional scarcity'. The last occasion these powers were actually employed was in the period November 1969 to March 1970 during a particularly severe winter.

Finding suitable secure places for visiting teams to stay and to train was another problem in a country where as perhaps a third of the surviving housing stock was still in some way war damaged, or in bad repair through neglect.

However, these problems were as nothing compared to the apparently intractable challenge of how to transport up to a hundred thousand spectators to the matches planned to take place at Wembley Stadium. Right up until May 1966 contingency plans were in place to switch some or all of these matches to either Northlands Road Ground in Southampton, Fratton Park in Portsmouth or even Ninian Park in Cardiff or one of the larger northern grounds already scheduled to stage matches that July.

Today we know that the regeneration of London began with the brake neck development of the Wembley Park area, the priority given to resurrecting rail and road connections into the district, and to linking it to the old, wreck transportation hubs deep in the dead zones of the metropolis. It was said at the time – and not believed - that nine-tenths of all the money and effort making Wembley Stadium a viable stage for the 1966 World Cup was actually spent elsewhere in north London, and that the focus of so much attention on the area facilitated the vital early re-connection of rail lines into the north west quadrant of London some twelve to eighteen months earlier than they would otherwise have been opened up, the establishment of a network reconstruction camps joined by old and new roads, and the first comprehensive ground surveys of the surrounding region.

For what it is worth, the surviving Organising Committee, Ministry of Supply and Cabinet Papers indicate that as little as one pound in five was expended repairing Wembley Stadium and its immediate environs (but accounting practices in that period had a lot more in common with 'back of a cigarette packet' record-keeping than anything we would accept as legitimate 'management accounts' today!).

Much of the vital infrastructure – incidentally as necessary to host major sporting events as to support normal day to day life - had already been revived in Poplar around West Ham United's home by the spring of 1965. The Royal Engineers had restored – initially just made safe - the so-called Boleyn ground at Upton Park and made it their advanced depot in the East End; initially as a fortress but then when the general security situation had improved and they had no longer needed a fortress from which to sally forth, a depot, from which roads into and out of East London, the docklands and to neighbouring districts were methodically cleared or driven through the seas of rubble. Additionally, by the spring of 1966 many of the deeper railway tunnels had been pumped out and the Royal Engineers were investigating how to get significant 'joined up' sections of the London Underground system north of the River Thames working again.

Overland travel across London was still a little problematic at that time. There were radioactive hotspots and many areas north and south of the Thames had been inundated. For example, the London Underground had slowly flooded in the months after the war; and large areas around Westminster had begun to be reclaimed by swamp and marsh. Additionally, the long-buried rivers of London had begun to erode and explore ways to break out of their long entombment beneath the streets.

Inevitably, the cause celebre of the tournament was to be the arrival of the Argentine footballers in England. Antonio Rattin and his team mates must have felt like men being driven into the Colosseum with the points of spears pricking their back between their shoulder blades!

As the first match drew closer the clamour for Argentina to be excluded became a howling tide of outrage as the previous year's horror stories of the Falkland Islanders' – the 'Kelpers' - exile and ordeal – began again to fill the pages of the papers, the airwaves and to dominate every public platform.

If the stories were to be believed – and even at the time many suspected that the litany of atrocities might not be quite as dreadful as people claimed – then Argentine servicemen, policemen and civilians had committed a litany of monstrous war crimes against prisoners of war and the civilian population of the Falklands Archipelago.

Viewed through the long lens of history we now know the real, shocking substance of the indictments against the invaders, the occupation force and the agents of the Junta in Argentina after the conclusion of hostilities in 1964. This is not the place to restate these matters; other than to say that no member of any Argentine sporting team, or diplomatic delegation would have been safe if allowed to walk unescorted on the streets of the United Kingdom during that era. Emotions ran strong, and there was no shortage of inflammatory rhetoric on either side of the debate.

The nightmare for the FA Tournament Organising Committee, and the Government which had invested so much treasure and prestige in the enterprise was a possible boycott by the South American teams.

Regardless of the consideration that, given the mood of the country, by any rational standards it was madness allowing Argentina to play in England; it was understood that if the Argentine was prevented from competing in the tournament then Brazil and the others would stay at home and the competition would no longer have been a 'World Cup'. In retrospect it is remarkable that Margaret Thatcher's Government steadfastly ignored public opinion at home calling for the banning of the 'Argie murderers', and maintained a dignified silence in the face of the 'unhelpful commentary' emanating from the Junta in Buenos Aires.

The Junta in Buenos Aires presented the participation of the national team in the 'English World Cup' as the implicit acceptance by the old imperial masters of *Las Malvinas* of its defeat. The Argentine military gloated, confident that history was on their side. One is bound to wonder what might have happened had the 'victors' settled for their 'victory' and thereafter gone out of their way not to tweak Albion's tale?

Needless to say, behind the scenes there were many in Government who were all for banning *La Celeste y blanca* – the 'white and the sky blue', as the Argentine football team was known at home – but in the end wiser counsels prevailed.

In Parliament Her Majesty's Loyal Opposition twice put forward motions demanding that the Argentine footballers should be denied entry to the United Kingdom.

'*We* are above that sort of thing!' The Prime Minister retorted to repeated jibes in the House of Commons. '*We* do not confuse sport with politics!'

7 | Wembley Way

Former Red Army Junior Sergeant Anatoly Saratov was one of many 'displaced persons' who had volunteered to work in one of the special duties companies recruited to make ready the stadia, and the surrounding infrastructure, of the venues for the 1966 World Cup Finals. In all some twenty companies – each mustering up to as many as one hundred and fifty men, and women – were deployed to work at or around the eight 'host' stadiums. The stories of the men and women who made up the 'World Cup Auxiliary' as the Royal Engineers classified its temporary civilian adjunct, have provided the framework for many socio-anthropological and socio-economic academic and popular histories of the early phases of the national reconstruction programme launched by Margaret Thatcher's Government in the second half of the 1960s.

The WCA later became the basis for the 'National Auxiliary Workers Service', a pool of skilled labour which moved between key reconstruction projects until its disbandment in 1987. However, even within the WCA, Anatoly Saratov's extraordinary story was remarkable, and the author makes no apology for pausing in the narrative of the footballing dramas of July 1966 to tell Anatoly's tale. It is very hard now to comprehend how unnatural, how extraordinarily mixed up and twisted the background to the tournament was, and if one man's story serves to illustrate the topsy-turvey, Alice in Wonderland through the looking glass realities of *that* world then it is probably Anatoly's.

Anatoly was a war baby born in April or May 1942 somewhere in the Saratov Oblast of the Soviet Union. He was probably only about three months old when a woman fleeing from the advancing German Army fleeing across the Volga River snatched him up from the arms of dying woman at the roadside. The woman had been shot through the abdomen and such wounds were a death sentence. With her last breaths she had pleaded for somebody to take her baby...

'Anatoly' was the name given to him at the orphanage in Chelyabinsk where he spent his first years, and

'Saratov' because that was where his existence had first been registered in the Soviet Union.

The author has employed the 'English' equivalent unit designation throughout Anatoly's story so as to not over-load the narrative with long, unwieldy Soviet nomenclature.

Anatoly had volunteered to join the Red Army, joined the Cadet Corps and aged seventeen found himself sent to the Moscow Military District to report for parachutist training. Even in old age he remained a lean, sinewy man, although only five feet six or seven in height in his younger and middle years he was preternaturally tough, a man who was accustomed to taking hard knocks and bouncing straight back up to his feet ready to carry on fighting. He had been perfectly at home in the rough and tumble, casually brutal life of a lowly soldier in the Red Army and taken immense pride in being accepted into the elite airborne forces.

At the time of the October war Anatoly was a corporal in the 73rd Airborne Regiment serving in the Sverdlovsk Military District. Throughout 1963 his unit was engaged on policing duties in Georgia and Azerbaijan, operating as normal infantry. In November 1963 the 73rd was deployed to Bulgaria, then to the Yugoslav border at the start of 1964. Thereafter, the 73rd was almost continuously engaged in bitter fighting against the 'Red Dawn insurgency' in Transylvania and later in and around Bucharest. The 73rd had been given two hours to 'go to ground' before the Red Air Force nuked the Rumanian capital to snuff out the 'counter-revolutionary betrayal' of its leadership, whom it seemed were about to conclude some kind of pact with the Americans.

Like fighting men in any army, Anatoly and his comrades only ever got a partial, distorted account of what was actually going on in the world beyond the confines of their immediate battlefield.

Elements of the 73rd had been sent to put down another counter-revolutionary insurgency in Istanbul.

That was when the 'shit really hit the fan', Anatoly would recall, smiling sadly.

'That was the dirtiest business of all. Just killing, really. Most of the city was on fire by the time we pulled out. Those Red Dawn maniacs had taken Istanbul and they weren't the sort of people you could negotiate with, so we killed them all. Them, their women, kids, too. None of us liked that but we had our orders.'

The 73rd Airborne Regiment had suffered so many casualties by then that it was amalgamated with another depleted regiment, the 58th while it was preparing to transfer to Greece where a Red Army invasion had stalled in the face of unexpected resistance.

'Then we got told we were invading Malta!'

Literally, the next day the 58/73rd Airborne and the survivors of several other similarly decimated parachute units were herded on a fleet of transport aircraft.

'It was chaos. We had no objectives. The Navy was going to bombard the shit out of the island's defences and as soon as we hit the ground, we were supposed to shoot at anything that moved. One officer told us that there were already so many Soviet agents on Malta that we'd be welcomed with open arms and all the fighting would be over by the time we jumped!'

Needless to say, things had not worked out that way.

Anatoly was shot while he was swinging beneath his billowing parachute high above what he later learned was the village of Kalkara. A bullet had shattered his left arm above the elbow and when he hit the ground, he had fractured his right ankle.

'I regained consciousness in the back of a lorry.'

He was in agony and there were dead and badly wounded men around him. Through the miasma of pain, he quickly realised that he was a prisoner. At the time he was in so much pain that a bullet in the neck would have been a merciful release.

'Then I heard women's voices. I felt hands, gentle hands, checking my body for other, unseen wounds. And one woman knelt beside me and began to stroke my face and whisper comforting words to me. The other woman was bossing the soldiers around; she got really angry when they dropped me on the ground outside the hospital!'

The face of the woman who had comforted him on that short, nightmarish, jolting journey to the nearest hospital – at Bighi high above the Grand Harbour and Kalkara Creek – had lived with him forever.

'I only discovered who she was when I saw her face in

the newspapers about a year later.'

The two young Maltese women who had protected and comforted wounded friend and foe alike that day in April 1964 had 'gone on to other things'. They were none other than the – by then - wife of the British Ambassador to the United States and her then sister-in-law Rosa, who had since married Commander Alan Hannay whom, at the time of the Battle of Malta in which Anatoly Saratov was so badly wounded, had been the Lieutenant Purser/Supply Officer of HMS Talavera.

Anatoly had written to Rosa Hannay care of the British Embassy in Philadelphia thanking her 'for my life'. He had thought he was dead and she had given him hope.

Although it would be many years before he met his angel of mercy again, his letter was to be the beginning of an enduring friendship.

Rosa Hannay's return letter did not reach Anatoly for over six weeks. It was a warm, chatty reply. She had filled in details of that day; how she and her 'sister Marija' had been given the job of 'deciding which men or women should be rushed immediately to the open air 'assessment area' where doctors decided who should be rushed to the over-whelmed operating theatres, and patched up other, horribly injured men and women as best they could as each ambulance arrived at RNH Bighi', and how Marija had had a 'polite disagreement' with two Royal Marines who had wanted one of their own 'lightly injured' friends to 'jump the queue' ahead of Anatoly.

The next letter he received from Philadelphia was from Lady Marija Calleja-Christopher herself. That lady's tone had been no less personable than her *sister's*.

The Ambassador's wife had explained that she had been a 'guinea pig' for exactly the sort of surgery that had probably saved his left arm, and that she was most keen to learn of his recovery while sympathising with him that 'sometimes your bones will ache'.

In his first year in captivity recovering from his injuries Anatoly had become fluent in English, although not so voluble in Maltese which despite his best efforts, he found...impossible.

He had initially been treated at the Royal Naval Hospital Bighi, undergoing three separate operations to rebuilt his upper left arm before transferring to the SS

Canberra, which was serving as a hospital ship for the less seriously ill and for those in the initial stages of recuperation and rehabilitation.

Once he, and other of his comrades had been admitted to RNH Bighi, he was – to his astonishment - treated like any other patient. Later, onboard the Canberra the British made a show of guarding their Russian prisoners but nobody doubted that if any man attempted to escape, he would probably be lynched long before help arrived.

The British had summarily executed any Red Army man they suspected of killing civilians or members of the garrison who had surrendered to them; but the blood-letting was finished by the time Anatoly fully returned to the world of the living.

Anatoly had remained on Malta some fifteen months, three months on the sick list, and another three on light duties during which time he had begun working as a translator for the Military Administration of the archipelago. The last eight months of his time on Malta he was designated as a 'non-combatant trustee', effectively allowed to come and go from his billet without restriction 'on licence'.

In his head he had ceased to be a soldier the moment he had hit the ground in April 1964; for him the war was over. Strictly speaking, a lot of the work he did for his captives on Malta was treachery; aiding and abetting the enemy but the kindness of Rosa Hannay, his personal angel of mercy, and later the fairness and well, decency, of the people into whose hands he had literally fallen, had changed...everything.

Of course, not all his fellow prisoners of war felt the same way but that was their problem, not his. By the end of his time on Malta he was virtually a free man so his transfer to England when the Canberra returned to Southampton had not been a thing, he was in any way looking forward to.

However, within days of landing in England the Army had processed him into a holding facility – Bushfield Camp - on the South Downs near Winchester, he discovered that although there were supposedly strict rules about non-fraternisation with enemy prisoners that the camp was no kind of prison. He was issued with a ration book, clothes coupons – 'how you dress is your business, Mr Saratov, but we expect all persons to maintain the highest possible standards of personal hygiene while in our care' – and informed that if he made himself available for 'suitable employment' he would be free to come and go as he pleased.

It seemed somebody in Malta had passed a letter to the Governor-General's Office confirming that 'Saratov, Anatoly, former Junior Sergeant, 58/73th Red Army Parachute Reg. is of proven good character and has of his own free will assisted to the best of his ability the work of the military administration...'

This commendation had accompanied him, and his file, to England and the upshot of this was that the hard-pressed authorities in Hampshire no longer considered him to be a prisoner of war.

If he wished to so do, he was free to go home.

Not that this was possible, or frankly, desirable since a man in his situation once captured by the enemy was forever considered suspect by his former countrymen.

'I said I wished to remain in England,' Anatoly told the author with smiling eyes.

Anatoly had worked on a farm south of Winchester at Otterbourne for several months, and briefly as a labourer in the nearby city after clerking in the camp commandant's office. His left arm ached maddeningly some nights; a thing that was easily borne because he knew how lucky he had been not to lose it.

The arm 'never really felt right again' but 'I got by' Anatoly would grin.

'I was the Company Commander's secretary at Wembley. Somebody had to deal with all the red tape the Ministry of Supply sent through and well, I discovered that I was good at that sort of thing. Me! Think of that! All I'd ever been trained to do was jump out of aeroplanes and shoot people! And there I was the chief bureaucrat in the Company tent on the corner of Olympic Way and Engineers Way!'

Those were happy days.

'It was when I was working at the Wembley Park Camp – about a week after I arrived - that I met my wife.'

It was Anatoly who told me the forgotten – or perhaps, more correctly, neglected – history of 'Wembley Way'.

'Everybody assumes that nice long road – about a third of a mile dead straight north to south linking Wembley Park Station pointing directly between the twin towers of the old Empire Stadium was built at the same time as the ground back in the nineteen twenties. Actually, Olympic Way – which everybody calls 'Wembley Way' – was laid down just in time for the 1948 London Olympics. Wembley was the main venue for the athletics events and the hockey and football finals in 1948. Soon after the end of the Second World War there were acute labour shortages in the United Kingdom; while at the same time there were several hundred thousand German prisoners of war in England in the period 1945-47 - at one point in 1946 there were over 400,000 German POWs in the United Kingdom, some 15,000 of whom eventually had opted to remain in Britain by the time repatriated to Germany was completed in July 1948 - and many Germans were engaged clearing rubble, repairing roads and notably on the land bringing in the immediate post-war harvests. This was a thing which sat badly in Parliament,' Anatoly recounted ruefully, for even after the passage of several decades he was sometimes astonished by *British sensibilities.* 'There were questions in the House querying whether the Ministry of Labour ought to be using slave labour!'

In the event about a hundred German POWs were employed in the gangs building the Olympic Way, and the plans to utilise the by then dwindling number of men held in England around the venues for the 1948 Summer Olympiad were quietly dropped.

'It wasn't love at first sight,' Anatoly admitted sheepishly, recounting his first meeting with his future wife. 'We walked into each other and everything we were carrying fell on the ground! Greta was very angry!'

The next day she sought Anatoly out and apologised.

And that was that; love at 'second sight'.

Greta Randall was a couple of years older than Anatoly, a civilian secretary/typist/clerk employed in the Royal Engineer's Transportation Office. Some years later she would work in Miriam Prior's 'New London Office', but that is another story!

Most of her street had been demolished by a V-2 rocket in January 1945; fortunately, her mother and father had been out at work and she had been, aged five, at school a little less than a quarter-of-a-mile away at the time, so: 'There was no harm done!'

Greta's father had been a draftsman and the family had resettled in the West Country after the Second War, where she and her three younger siblings had all survived at Cheltenham.

Anatoly and Greta's first 'date' had come about when she asked him if he would escort her to nearby Dollis Hill because she had promised her parents that she would try to find their old home while she was working at Wembley Park.

It was an unlikely tryst; a walk through a shattered and burned landscape that was to cement a life-long partnership.

Greta would be three months pregnant with their first child that afternoon of 23rd July 1966 when she and Anatoly – newly married - took their seats in the South Stand of the Commonwealth Stadium to watch the World Cup Final.

8 | The Contenders

From the moment the Football Association promulgated – 'announced' simply does not do it justice – its right and intention to stage the World Cup of 1966, there were howls of anguish in the Iberian Peninsula, Italy and throughout South America.

The Spanish had provoked and lost a very unpleasant naval and air war against the British in December 1963 and they and their Generalissimo who was still hiding in his bunker beneath the Royal Alcazar of Madrid, were still smarting from the rough treatment meted out to them.

The Italians – it was ridiculous to pretend there was any sort of coherent government of the half let alone the whole of Italy at this time – felt mightily aggrieved that the perfidious British had not come to their aid; conveniently forgetting that the reason nobody would treat with the feuding factions in Rome or Naples or Florence or Venice, and that the Royal Navy and RAF periodically harried Sicilian pirates in the narrows seas between that island and Tunisia, was that the Regia Aeronautica had sunk British ships and murdered hundreds of people in a sneak attack on Malta.

It was one of those bizarre oddities that sport throws up that the one thing most Italians actually united behind was not a common flag or political philosophy; but their national football team in which men from all over the country, who otherwise would be shouldering rifles and standing ready to shoot their neighbours, were perfectly at ease playing football in 'Italian' colours.

Not that Spain – Franco's fascist Spain – was any less a collection of ancient kingdoms reluctantly drawn together whose peoples regarded themselves as Andalusians, Castilians or Catalans, Basques or Galicians and so on, before they called themselves 'Spaniards'.

At least in footballing terms Great Britain had hived off the constituent nations of its Union into England, Scotland, Wales and Northern Ireland, although within that loyalties to club – Manchester United, Blackburn Rovers, Sheffield Wednesday, West Bromwich Albion or whatever - were probably as passionate as any Castilian's was for his native Castile, or Spain.

Humankind is a tribal polity; rarely more so than on a football field. However, the Spanish and the Italians were never going to be the first to pull out, no matter how aggrieved their fractured, enfeebled governments at home were with the English. Often in time of trouble nations attempt to find strength, solidarity in gestures, sometimes religious, sometimes temporal and in sport the two are often combined. Moreover, for the Spanish and the Italians the World Cup was a priceless opportunity for the diplomats who accompanied their sporting ambassadors to England to re-open long severed lines of communication with clearly, indisputably the most powerful surviving Western European country, and whether they liked it or not the last best hope for maintaining some kind of stability in the Mediterranean.

Argentina and its Latin American bedfellows; Brazil, Uruguay, Mexico, Colombia and a little half-heartedly, Chile had threatened to boycott the tournament several times. All six, barring Chile were heavily dependent on United States financial, economic and military aid. Chile was different because it had never really thrown off its links with Great Britain, or the Royal Navy and it had chaffed that American aid, which it still badly needed for the reconstruction following the Valdivia earthquake of 1960 was the work of a generation, was increasingly dependent on Chilean diplomatic and political alignment with the whims of successive US Administrations, and liable to stop and start without warning. On top of this Chile and Argentina had an old and unresolved dispute over the Magellan Strait and other, unsettled border disputes. Oh, and the two countries did not, and never had liked each other...

Nonetheless, the Latin American countries formed a threatening block whose withdrawal could at any time turn the tournament into a charade.

The first argument – actually, a flaming row – had been over who exactly should be invited to England in 1966. The *Confederación Sudamericana de Fútbol* – the South American Football Confederation (known by the acronym CONMEBOL), and The Confederation of North, Central American and Caribbean Association Football (CONCACAF), the latter for the most part lightly affected and the former not at all inconvenienced by the unpleasantness over those Cuban missiles in late 1962, had gone ahead with their respective qualifying tournaments for the 1966 World Cup.

Obviously, this had not been feasible in the United Kingdom or Europe and many of the teams which might otherwise have attempted to qualify represented countries like Poland, Czechoslovakia, East and West Germany which no longer existed, or were in no fit state to field sides, like France, Belgium, the Netherlands, Austria, Yugoslavia, Greece, and so on.

The South Americans had no sympathy for this.

None whatsoever.

While England as the hosts had an automatic right to play in the tournament; in South and Central American eyes the other eight European teams and the single African country invited to participate did not. What particularly angered the 'Latin contingent' was that the Football Association had issued its invitations unilaterally without consultation with *anybody* else.

Oddly, since most of the 'Latin Countries' were ruled by despots; it ought to have come as no surprise to them that the Football Association - also ruled by despots – albeit of a kind no less vindictive, but thankfully lacking armies and police forces slavishly at their command, would behave in any other way.

Ted Dexter was appalled when the Foreign and Commonwealth Office let him have sight of some of the diplomatic notes filling the Secretary of State's in-box in January 1966.

The FA had high-handedly sent out the invitations without bothering to tell the Minister of Sport what it was doing, and without discussing the matter with *anybody*; as if in the post-October War World its first major global sporting event was nothing whatsoever to do with politics.

'I was called into the FCO and given a frightful wigging by Lord Harding-Grayson,' the former England Cricket Captain recollected. 'Oh, don't get me wrong. He was very civil, and I think a little bit amused by the whole thing but it was very much a head of school-mischievous schoolboy meeting and I wondered at several points whether my time in government was about to come to a sticky end. 'Those beggars at the Football Association have pulled a fast one on you,' he said. 'Be a good fellow, don't let it happen again.'

Dexter had inquired what the Secretary of State was going to do about 'those beastly telegrams?'

'Oh those,' the great man had sighed. 'Don't worry about those. I'll deal with them.'

In fact, Lord Harding-Grayson played the only cards available. He let it be known to the Argentine Junta that he was the only 'sane' voice in Oxford and that but for him Royal Navy submarines would at that very moment be blockading all ports and attacking, without warning any warship which dared to put to sea.

'I do not want another war but you need to understand I am a lone voice in Oxford and if you undermine me well...on your own head be it!'

By then fifty-seven-year old Arturo Frondizi Ercoli, the man occupying La Casa Rosado – 'The Pink House' – the home and the office of the President of the Argentine in the role of the military's democratic fig leaf and his fellow Junta members thought Margaret Thatcher and most of her ministers were barking mad. No matter what they said at home to their own people, or to whoever was willing to listen to them in Philadelphia, the Argentine leadership had breathed a huge collective sigh of relief when disasters elsewhere had compelled the British to lift the submarine blockade of Las Malvinas and the Argentine seaboard the previous July. For all that they had 're-conquered Las Malvinas' and successfully deported the population once the British submarines had arrived in the South Atlantic the Junta's victory had profited it little and had the 'war' continued much longer, the economy of the coastal zone from the mouth of the River Plate to Tierra del Fuego would have collapsed. There might well have been a popular uprising against the regime, a civil war with various factions of the military at odds...

From where Ercoli sat in the Casa Rosado the thought of the Army and the Navy and the Air Force, each of which mistrusted, and basically loathed, the other services being drawn into open conflict as the self-appointed agents of the competing entrenched political and economic vested interest groups in the Republic was a nightmare.

In fact, it hardly bore thinking about...

Unlike many of his colleagues in Government Tom Harding-Grayson never mistook Argentine bellicosity for strength; thus, in reminding the Junta in Buenos Aires that he was the one who had called the ceasefire in July 1964 and that he was the one who might, at any time, release again the dogs of war – half-a-dozen advanced 'O' and 'P' class diesel-electric submarines – into South Atlantic waters, he effectively held the men in 'the Pink House' in the palm of his hand in the lead up to the tournament.

'I suppose,' Dexter reminisced, 'given all the other things on Lord Harding-Grayson's plate at the time my little *footballing* problems were very small beer. Possibly, a little bit of light relief!'

Nevertheless, the high-handed attitude of the Football Association caused a raft of wholly avoidable difficulties and left a legacy of ill-will that still resonates globally and probably explains why England have never again come close – never actually even been in the running – to being awarded the Finals a second time.

The invitation to Ghana, probably the best team in Africa was only mildly contentious; no more than a starting point for the chorus of South American complaint. The problem was not really with the inclusion of Spain, Italy, Portugal, Sweden and Switzerland; most of whom might have qualified in the normal course of events. No, the real point – or rather, three points – of contention was that Scotland, Wales and Northern Ireland had all been given wildcards.

The continual bickering eventually produced a stand-off and the Football Association – entirely ignorant of the Foreign and Commonwealth Secretary, Lord Thomas Carlyle Harding-Grayson's carefully choreographed stealthy intervention to keep 'Argentina in its cage' - became the unlikely beneficiaries of raw realpolitik. It goes without saying that Sir Stanley Rous and Harold Thompson proudly proclaimed how they had 'faced down' the recalcitrant 'Latins', ignorant both of the Foreign and Commonwealth Secretary's quiet machinations or the Prime Minister's high-level conversations with her Portuguese, Swedish and Swiss counterparts, and via emissaries with both the Spanish and Italians (both of whom were intent on 'not antagonising' the Angry Widow).

While the Latin Americans stood together, they were but six voices and from the outset England could count on the support of Scotland, Wales and Northern Ireland (a thing rarely to be repeated in footballing terms in later years). Which left the five European entrants, and Ghana, which categorically refused to take sides, thereby alienating the footballing tyrants in both Europe and Latin America for many years thereafter. In the end all five European football associations sided with the FA.

Less than a month before the opening match, scheduled for the evening of Monday the 4th July 1966 between England and Chile at Wembley Stadium, the FA informed the dissenters, led by Argentina that if they boycotted or disrupted the competition then European teams would do likewise in 1970 when the tournament was due to be held in the Americas.

Threatened with an endless cycle of boycotts invalidating the whole idea, and the intrinsic worth of the World Cup, Brazil, then Chile, within a day or two Mexico and Colombia, and finally Uruguay and Argentina publicly stepped back from the brink.

Needless to say, the bitterness of the disputes behind the scenes inevitably leeched onto the field but that is to get ahead of ourselves. It was only late in the day that talk of football started to dominate the back pages of the national newspapers.

When eventually thoughts turned to the actual football it was generally accepted that Brazil were the team to beat – although not many people thought that was possible – and that Italy, or perhaps another of the South American teams, Argentina principally were viewed as huge obstacles to all of the Home Countries.

While both Wales and Northern Ireland had a sprinkling of gifted performers – the Irish had George Best, let it not be forgotten – Scotland were the competition's dark horses. Predicting the form of the runners was however, a bit of a mug's game because none of the Home Countries had played regularly since the October War until that spring, and although the Football Association had arranged charity matches between scratch 'Manchester', 'Sheffield' and 'Birmingham' elevens against and experimental England side that spring, and Scotland had played similar fixtures against Glasgow, Edinburgh and Rest of Scotland elevens starting the previous autumn, few conclusions could realistically be drawn from these contests. Wales and Northern Ireland had played similar fixtures against a Glaswegian combination and against Hearts and Hibernian in Edinburgh respectively in May.

Theoretically, England had home advantage and the Scots, Welsh and the Ulstermen were hardly 'playing away' in foreign conditions; so that had to count for something but nobody really knew. However, whereas European international soccer had ceased – hardly a surprise – in October 1962 and only started to resume, very much around the edges of the shattered continent the previous year; the Latin Americans had never stopped fulfilling fixtures against each other.

Only in the Iberian Peninsula had domestic football carried on uninterrupted – after a brief hiatus in November and December 1962. In England normal football had only fully resumed – on a and then on a semi-professional basis in the lower leagues - in in England in the 1965-66 season. It was different for the Scots because their leagues, suspended in the winter of 1962-63, had restarted in their pre- October 1962 format in the autumn of 1963 and got back to what passed for 'normal' during that season, well over a year before its southern counterparts.

For England the great imponderable was that Division 1, the top tier of the Football League had been robbed of seven of its teams, and the lower leagues likewise decimated. All the London teams were gone: 'Spurs', the double winning maestros of Tottenham Hotspur; 'the Gunners', Arsenal; 'the Hammers', West Ham United; Fulham; Leyton Orient; and also, a Chelsea side that had looked likely to walk back into the top flight that season. Moreover, the two great Merseyside rivals, Liverpool and Everton whose grounds separated by Stanley Park still stood – seemingly intact from a distance but close up, cracked and crumbling, blackened by thermal shock - amidst the devastation of the surrounding city but their playing staffs and most of their supporters had been wiped out on the night of the October War. A third of the clubs in top two tiers of the

English game, and approximately the same proportion of its players had died in the war or since; a ratio tragically in line with the population 'die off' across England in those years immediately following the cataclysm.

Eight of the twenty-two men who had travelled to Chile in the summer of 1962 were dead; or more accurately, had perished, or disappeared, not one of whom had a known grave. The roll of honour reads like a who's who of the stalwarts of the England team and its coming men:

Name	Club	Age	Fate
Ramon Wilson	Huddersfield Town	27	Last seen alive 15/12/62.
Gerry Hitchens	Inter Milan	28	Last seen alive 12/1/63 (Milan).
James Greaves	Tottenham Hotspur	22	Presumed killed 28/10/62.
Johnny Haynes	Fulham	27	Presumed killed 28/10/62.
George Eastham	Arsenal	26	Presumed killed 28/10/62.
Maurice Norman	Tottenham Hotspur	28	Presumed killed 28/10/62.
Roger Hunt	Liverpool	24	Presumed killed 28/10/62.
Robert Moore	West Ham United	21	Thought to have died of his injuries 29/10/62.

Conceivably, all these men might have been a key part of, or at least in contention for places in Alf Ramsey's 1966 England squad. And coming up behind them what of all the young aspirants whose lives, careers and futures were snuffed out in an instant by the great thermonuclear blooms over London and the other cities of England?

How many careers were blighted by the privations of the immediate post-war years, with unknown, unknowing brushes with radioactive hotspots, fallout and disease?

There was much talk in the spring of 1966 about the example of Manchester United and the 'Busby Babes' after the Munich Air Crash in 1958; a discussion given extra piquancy by the fact that United had pipped Sheffield Wednesday, Blackpool and Leeds United to win the Division 1 title in early May by a single point. Many of United's stars, including England's 'midfield wizard'

Bobby Charlton and pugnacious 'stopper' Nobby Stiles, Scotland's goal thief Denis Law, and Northern Ireland's rising star, George Best, were confidently expected to feature prominently in the coming tournament.

However, Manchester United had recovered, 'united' in every way by adversity yet in a world that was otherwise still intact. The club's legendary manager Matt Busby had been able to bring in, and to buy in men to replace his fallen 'babes', to rebuild from still firm foundations, with his teams willed on to greatness by its unscathed fanatical supporters.

Manchester United's tragedy had been a single air crash on a snowy night in Munich; England's catastrophe had been a global disaster of unprecedented magnitude.

The October War had torn a huge chunk out of England and the national game; so many were gone, so much had been lost and nobody really thought England had any real chance of progressing much farther than the group stages of the Finals.

England's heroes had hardly played together; many of the men Alf Ramsey was to send out to battle were, in comparison to the South American stars, callow and inexperienced at the highest level and had never, ever encountered men with the extravagant skills of the Brazilians, or the Portuguese or the Argentines.

In fact, many rated Scotland's chances better; the Scots were a team of free spirits including a handful of men whose talents would have sat happily within the Brazilian set-up. Built around the nucleus of Celtic and Rangers stalwarts; with Jim Baxter pulling the strings in midfield, Jimmy Johnstone weaving confusion on the wing, Manchester United's Paddy Crerand, Celtic's Billy McNeill and Ranger's John Greig like gatekeepers in defence and Denis Law up front poaching goals for fun the Scots, not England, were most pundits 'most likely outsiders'.

Critics pointed to the Scots' lack of depth; yes, the first eleven was formidable but what if somebody got injured or lost form? But footballers were harder men then than they are now, accustomed to playing with knocks and niggles that would put a present-day player on the treatment table for a month. And besides, that perceived 'lack of depth' was illusory, unlike in England the conveyor belt of youngsters coming up through the ranks had never stopped, let alone stalled and one of the things which motivated the Scots first team men of that age was the knowledge that there were always young guns aplenty snapping at their heels.

Moreover, in forty-three-year old John 'Jock' Stein, the former Celtic player and manager of Hibernian, Scotland had possibly the most formidable managerial personality of any of the sixteen teams in the World Cup Finals of 1966. The tournament was to be his swansong as national manager; he had already signed a contract to manage Glasgow Celtic that autumn and in the year that he had been in charge of the Scottish team many people believed he had done the impossible, welded the disparate spirits, and wayward genius of several of his men into a 'real team' for the first time in years.

In February 1966 at Hampden Park in front of perhaps as many as one hundred and twenty thousand ecstatic supporters Scotland had walloped England 5-2. It could have been eight or nine nil but for sloppy defending and a second-half display that Jock Stein had later derisively described as 'show-boating'. Yes, his settled eleven had been up against a makeshift team – Alf Ramsey had given several men a debut, to 'see what they are made of' – and an ankle injury to full back Don Howe had, in that era when there were no substitutes in international matches, made a nonsense of the England manager's 4-3-3 system. Even so had Ramsey been in any doubt as to the scale of the challenge before him the match would have unambiguously disabused him of that notion.

England had won both the other matches of the British Championship that spring, finishing second in the table. Meanwhile, Scotland had won 3-1 in Belfast against Northern Ireland and beaten the Welsh 2-1 at home in a desultory, off-colour performance during which they had trailed the Welsh for nearly sixty minutes.

All that seemed a little academic; the Brazilians were coming and everybody understood that Pelé and company were like nothing English shores had ever seen before!

Well, certainly not since the visit of Ferenc Puskas and his incomparable Hungarians had come to England in 1953 and won 6-3 at Wembley!

9 | England in July 1966

Practically everything Alf Ramsey had done in the season of 1965-66 had been cautious, measured and well, boring. He spoke – always briefly, tersely, with polite indifference – about being ready for the 'opening match' in July 1966. He said 'it would be nice to win every game in the run-up to the competition' but 'that pre-supposes a preparation period of years, rather than months'.

To stop Ramsey accepting one of the many offers of employment back in the Football League he had been appointed the Football Association's Head of Coaching; albeit at half his Manager's salary in July 1963. In one sense the 'lost years' had not been wasted because his FA post enabled him to spend weeks on end on the training grounds of English clubs assessing and coaching players who would later appear in the 1966 squad.

Ramsey, now forty-six years old, had effectively been England's manager in waiting for the best part of four years – four years in which he would otherwise have been planning, plotting, experimenting and building *his* World Cup-winning team – rather than finding himself with less than six months in which to cobble together whatever could be 'cobbled together' before the opening match of the tournament.

His first full international match as England Manager was the now infamous drubbing at Hampden Park; a fixture he had asked the FA to arrange as a 'warm-up' in June, not the frost of February. But then Ramsey had asked for the Home International Championship to be re-started after, not before the World Cup.

'I learned more from the matches against club and *City* fixtures than I did from the Scottish, Welsh or Northern Ireland matches," Ramsey was to claim. I knew there were plenty of good players in England, the problem was identifying the ones who would fit into the system I planned to play and had the mental strength to perform in the heat of the coming World Cup. The secret was in playing men, wherever possible, in their club positions and in making them understand that what I wanted from them was not *England* performances but their *club* performances. The Home Internationals were a waste of time; all they achieved was to allow three of our possible opponents in the coming tournament to have a good look at us!'

After the humiliation of the Hampden Park match, he was deadpan, almost sanguine: 'I have learned more today than I would have if we had fought out a goalless draw, or we had won or lost by a single goal.'

The FA Council had given him no support whatsoever in organising the sort of fixtures Ramsey wanted and several of the big clubs had reported men injured at the last minute, or simply refused to release them for England's 'practice matches' that spring.

It was ever thus in English football...

Ramsey never complained; he had known what he was getting himself into going to work for the Football Association in 1962.

Constantly, the England manager was pressed as to how he rated his team's chances.

'I believe that we will progress to the knock out stages of the tournament. After that, every side has a chance of progressing further...'

People forgot that this was the same Alf Ramsey who had led Ipswich Town from the Third Division (South) to the Division 1 Championship in no time flat, and that when he had been appointed to the top job by the Football Association in the autumn before the fall he had been, and presumably still was, the obvious if not the only man, for the herculean task before him.

When one journalist put to him in the week before the opening match that 'the phoney war is about to end', Ramsey had momentarily lost his temper.

'We are playing a football match next week, not fighting a damned war!'

That was it, the one flash of intemperance.

Ramsey could be different behind the closed dressing room door; although he was no 'shouter', and not the man to belittle one of his men in front of his fellows. If he had a fault it was that when he took a dislike to a man, or gave up on him, that was that and there was usually no way back.

Many of his players thought he was old-fashioned, mocked his accent – elocution lessons had transformed his East London childhood accent into clipped received

BBC English over the years – and sometimes resented, or simply did not understand his tactical schemes. Ramsey was a thinker, a man who questioned the old precepts of formation, kick and charge which had dominated the English game from time immemorial. He knew his men could not match, man for man, the extravagant skills of the Brazilians, or even on a bad day, the extrovert antics of the Scots but that was nothing to panic over. If he could not over-power sides by muscle, sweat, pure bravura in the traditional 'English way' then perhaps his teams might play in ways that negated the brilliance of its foes, perhaps the 'system' might compensate for shortcomings in other respects?

The 4-3-3 system was not new.

After the 1945 war everybody had still played 2-3-5: two full backs, left and right; three defensive midfielders, left-half, centre-half and right-half; and five attackers, wingers to the left and right, two inside forwards and a centre forward, with either the wingers or more likely the inside forwards being expected to track back and help out in midfield at need. It was a system of movement which inevitably left gaps, or space for the opposition to move into or play through.

4-3-3 was different: with four dedicated defenders in a flat line in the thirty to forty yards in front of the goalkeeper. Each man 'marked space' and thus denied it to the opposition, with two central defenders, one to the left, one to the right ready to cover the left and right full backs on the flanks. In midfield there was scope for the central man of the three-man line to fall back into a traditional centre half role or to 'hold' the ball in the middle of the park, likewise the flanking left and right-halves could mark the space ahead of the full backs or move forward to assist in attack. Up front one man might be a traditional winger, another a traditional inside forward, and usually, there would be just the one man operating in and around the opponents' penalty area as an old-fashioned centre forward-striker.

The down side of 4-3-3 was that it demanded a wider range of specialised skills and aptitudes from individual players, it required players to work in co-ordinated groups and it was essentially defensive. By leaving the defence to mark space and midfielders and forwards to track back and 'pick up' their opposite numbers when they came forward, it also increased workloads and demanded greater physical fitness and stamina. In an era before substitutes it was not unusual to see sides troop of the pitch in a virtual state of collapse, the last quarter of a match having been played at a walking pace due to the exhaustion of the majority of the players.

The substitution of a single player on account of his having suffered a demonstrably 'serious injury' had been introduced in the Football League in the 1965-66 season. Such a rule was considered for the international game by FIFA after the 1966 World Cup and then amended ahead of the 1970 tournament due to be held at altitude in hot conditions to permit up to 2 substitutions for any reason.

Nevertheless, as systems went, 4-3-3 had a host of advantages for a team in England's position. For one, if everybody knew what they were doing it made it very hard for the opposition to dance through one's ranks like a hot knife through butter. At the very least anybody coming up against one of Ramsey's teams operating a well-co-ordinated 4-3-3 formation was going to be in for a fight. Admittedly, there was nothing Ramsey or anybody else could do if a team playing an exquisite touch and go, pinpoint first time passing game succeeded in playing through and around his team but, on balance, he did not think that was likely to happen that often and pragmatist to the core, he was solely focused on making the best possible fist of things with the resources he had at his disposal.

Critics hold – wrongly in this author's opinion – that most England managers throughout history had such a wealth of talent to pick from that they could have fielded three or four teams as good as, or better than the one they actually selected on any given day. Many point out that despite the ravages of the war Ramsey was spoilt for choice, albeit among a generation of surviving professional footballers who were of a uniformly high, but not necessarily world-beating standard.

But that was the problem, of course.

England had plenty of 'good players' but hardly a wealth of world-beaters.

Ahead of the tournament possibly only Bobby Charlton, or goalkeeper Gordon Banks might have seriously contested a place – on the reserve bench at least – in a World XI of the period. That said, no man needed to tell Ramsey that in most circumstances an individual was as nothing to 'the team'. In fact, he mistrusted 'stars', other than those of the modest, self-effacing hard-working sort like Charlton. At this remove people too readily forget that Ramsey was a manager who had built his reputation on his ability to get the very best out of men who had never quite reached the heights under other managers.

Thus, when he unveiled his final twenty-two at the end of May 1966 there were more than a few raised eyebrows. Solid, staid, unimaginative Alf Ramsey had, to the consternation and delight of the pundits pulled a series of selectorial rabbits out of a hat.

The England squad for the 1966 World Cup Finals was drawn from thirteen clubs with an average age of around twenty-seven (a year older than the squad in Chile in 1962).

Of that Chilean squad there were nine survivors: goalkeepers Ron Springett (Sheffield Wednesday) and Alan Hodgkinson (Sheffield United); full backs Jimmy Armfield (Blackpool) and Don Howe (West Bromwich Albion); centre half Peter Swan (Sheffield Wednesday); midfielders Ron Flowers (Wolverhampton Wanderers) and Bobby Charlton (Manchester United); and forwards John Connelly (Burnley) and Derek Kevan (West Bromwich Albion).

Of those nine men only four had played in any of the games in Chile: Springett, Armfield, Flowers and Charlton.

There was no dissent about the third keeper in the squad; and everybody assumed Gordon Banks (Leicester City) would be the man 'between the sticks' in the opening match of the tournament against Chile at Wembley on 4th July.

Nor was there any real surprise that full backs Bobby Thomson (Wolverhampton Wanderers) and Keith Newton (Blackburn Rovers) were also named. There were nods of approval from all when Nobby Stiles (Manchester United) was confirmed in the twenty-two. Nobody cavilled at the inclusion of both Jack Charlton – elder brother of Bobby – and his youthful club mate Norman Hunter (Leeds

United) alongside Gerry Young (Sheffield Wednesday) as central defenders alongside Peter Swan. Both Charlton and Hunter were rock-like 'stoppers', although the former was a menace in attack in the air, and the latter – his brutal tackling apart – was known to have an underused, but nonetheless, 'intelligent and deft' left foot.

The real 'turnups' came in the selections higher up the field.

Michael O'Grady (Huddersfield Town) and uncapped Peter Eustace (Sheffield Wednesday) were classy midfielders with an eye for goal who had only featured in a single trial match, against a scratch Birmingham – combined Birmingham City and Aston Villa side – in May.

Ramsey only named two wingers in the squad: Terry Paine (Southampton), a veteran in comparison with Alan Ball (Blackpool).

Only two wingers!

What was the world coming to?

England had struggled to score goals in all the warm up and British Championship matches; relying on Bobby Charlton trademark thunderbolts from range and goals from free kicks and corner kicks in the main to squeeze out results or snatch unlikely draws.

Either or both of John Connelly and Derek Kevan had been on most people's team sheet for the opening match against Chile for some months; so, when the last two names on Alf Ramsey's squad list came out of the hat for some seconds people who were there at the news conference recollected 'you could have heard a pin drop'. Before, of course, pandemonium erupted.

Geoff Hurst, the former West Ham United forward who had survived the night of the war with relatively minor injuries and signed for Southampton mid-way through the abbreviated 1963-64 season had been scoring goals for fun ever since, had been given a couple of run outs but been dropped – and apparently discarded - after the Scotland fiasco.

Nobody had even mentioned the name of thirty-one-year old Sunderland striker Brian Howard Clough…

Which was, in retrospect a little odd, because to this day nobody who has played over three hundred matches in the English Football league has ever scored goals with such consistent, metronomic frequency.

On the day his name caused such consternation in the press room of the newly re-opened Empire Stadium - Most of the rest of the Stadium was still a building site at that stage (less than three-months from the opening match) - Clough had scored 321 goals in 339 senior adult and cup matches for Middlesbrough, and latterly, Sunderland. By and large he had been ignored by England, having played the last of his two matches for the national side as long ago as 1959.

The thing that most astonished the reporters in that room was that if they, as a group, had been asked to describe exactly the sort of player that Alf Ramsey had never tolerated, or been remotely interested in coaching, or having anywhere near one of *his* teams, to a man the press corps would have chorused the name BRIAN CLOUGH.

The man was tough as nails, sharp enough to cut himself, and even cockier. He was one of those rare, remarkable men who is pathologically incapable of keeping his mouth shut when his life depends upon it. Authority brought the worst out in him; and like many Yorkshireman before, and after him, he was hard-wired to automatically pick a fight with the strongest character in any dressing room.

For a centre-forward he was not overly physically prepossessing, hardly intimidating at a lithely built five feet and ten inches in height. On the field he was not gifted with lightning speed or reflexes, and sometimes he was invisible, a passenger. Until, that was, the ball came in his direction when he was anywhere near the opponents' goal.

And then he was electric, the ultimate cold-eyed gunslinger, nerveless and precise invariably striking with Cobra-like speed and precision. Moreover, when he struck it was invariably with a suicidal commitment that paid no heed to flying boots or bodies, regardless of the mud of a turnip patch pitch or a winter's frost lying cruelly on the ground.

In June 1966 people were saying that the man who had scored so many goals was approaching the twilight of his career, one injury away from retirement.

10 | The Lay of the Land

How can one put it *diplomatically*?

Tricky...

Football in the 1960s was not as we know it today; either on or off the field and the particular circumstances of *that* World Cup tournament added another twist to the story.

Normally, FIFA would have appointed its people to the Organising Committee overseeing the footballing carnival. It would have had the last word on everything, including the draw for the group stage, the venues, appointed all the match officials and acted as judge and jury in all matters of player discipline. FIFA's Organising Committee would not have got everything right but it would have been, on the face of it, *neutral*.

In 1966 FIFA only existed in its 'Roman' incarnation which was neither representative, or in any way neutral and generally, scorned by the Football Associations of fifteen of the sixteen finalists. One solution to the problem of 'bias' and 'partiality' in the organisation and administration of the tournament might have been to draw the membership of the *English* Football Association's Organising Committee from representatives of all sixteen finalists. But this was not what happened; in fact, the FA did not even consider such a 'democratic' option.

'There was no time for any of that!' Sir Stanley Rous argued.

Even at the time there were people – not in the FA, obviously – who thought this sounded a little like: 'We know best,' and 'We can't be bothered to take anybody else's opinions, worries or interests into account!'

Quite apart from the difficulties this would create for English – and by association, the Scottish, Welsh and Irish down the years – the FA's arrogant abrogation of all FIFA powers to itself was to unnecessarily complicate and undermine its moral authority, and its governance of the 1966 tournament.

While the FA mandated the manner of the draw, the venues at which matches would be played, the schedule and the composition of the list of officials who would referee and run the lines throughout the tournament; not even the FA at the height of its hubris made provision for a 'disciplinary panel' to sit during the Finals.

Basically, nobody took responsibility for 'discipline' at the 1966 tournament; and needless to say, whatever the rights or wrongs of the FA's abdication; nobody has ever made the same mistake again.

Within the FA Sir Stanley subsequently claimed that: 'If we'd taken responsibility many disgraceful episodes would have been punished and subsequent ones thereby avoided!'

Harold Thompson later said: 'I felt we ought to have taken responsibility for this...' However, at the time he was at best *agnostic* about the FA taking *responsibility* for enforcing disciplinary sanctions on 'foreign teams' who might elect, 'as is their right, to defy us.'

John Joe Mears, who as Chairman of the FA had the casting vote in any matter falling under the remit of the tournament Organizing Committee flatly refused to touch the 'discipline area' with a barge pole.

'The English FA had no authority over the conduct of the players of other international teams!'

In this, as in other things, the former Chairman of Chelsea Football Club was probably the calm voice of sanity.

'We had no choice but to take control of practically everything else,' he was to recollect, 'otherwise the tournament simply would not have happened. 'Yes, we made a lot of mistakes. We should have tried to get more consensus about which referees refereed which matches, and so forth. The tournament ought to have been held over a longer period, but the 'discipline thing', well, without FIFA operating as a World governing body, which it was not in 1966, we could not act as judge and jury in our own court. That just would not have been right.'

To be fair to the Organising Committee, they got a lot of things right. Or at least as 'right' as anybody could have got them in the singular circumstances of 1966.

To ensure that not all the best teams were pitted against each other in one of the four qualifying groups which decided the quarter-final line-up; each of the sixteen teams had been 'seeded' in one of four 'draw groups' for 'the draw' in Birmingham on Friday 7th May, the evening before the FA Cup Final (Won by Sheffield Wednesday 3-2 against Manchester United).

With the Empire Stadium not at that time being deemed ready to host that occasion the Football Association caravan had moved to the home of Aston Villa, Villa Park in the Midlands to hold the World Cup preliminaries and the highlight of the footballing year.

The four *strongest* teams had arbitrarily – but not unreasonably - been deemed to be Brazil, Argentina, England and Italy; the second rank of teams was Scotland, Portugal, Uruguay and Spain; the third Chile, Switzerland, Wales and Northern Ireland; and the weakest nations Ghana, Mexico, Sweden and Colombia.

How on earth Mexico and Sweden got to be allocated to the fourth rank, beggars belief; never mind, the thought processes of footballing grandees down the years have always been a mystery to most of us!

The draw was further complicated by the fact that it was decided that none of the 'Home Countries' should be drawn in the same qualifying group. Apparently, this had nothing to do with geography or footballing considerations it was simply because one of the South American teams registered an objection on the grounds that it was likely that one of England, Scotland, Wales or Northern Ireland might 'throw' a match in order to in some way 'rig' the quarter-final line-up.

The format of the tournament was that the Group's would be numbered 1 to 4; the group winners and the runners up both going through to the quarter-final stage.

Additionally – again because of the fears of certain participants that the competition might be gerrymandered in favour of England or the other Home Countries, lots were drawn to determine which group's winner and which group's runner up would contest which quarter-final ahead of the draw.

The Quarter-Finals would all kick off at 3:00 PM on Saturday 16th July.

Quarter-Final no. 1 would be contested by the winner of Group 1 and the runner up in Group 2.

Quarter-Final no. 2 would be contested by the winner of Group 3 and the runner up of Group 4.

Quarter-Final no. 3 would be contested by the winner of Group 2 and the runner up of Group 1.

Quarter-Final no. 4 would be contested by the winner of Group 4 and the runner up of Group 3.

All this mattered because thereafter the winners of Quarter-Finals no. 1 and no. 2 would contest Semi-Final no. 1; and the winners of Quarter-Finals no. 3 and no. 4 would contest Semi-Final no. 2.

For reasons nobody has ever explained Semi-Final no. 2 was scheduled to be played on the evening of Tuesday 19th July; and Semi-Final no. 1 would be played the next evening. Both Semi-finals would kick off at 7:30 PM.

If England qualified for the quarter-final or the semi-final stage those matches would be played at Wembley. Footballing mythology holds that this also was objected to but the Organising Committee wisely ignored all protests.

'Making England play anywhere else would have been a nonsense,' John Joe Mears remarked as the repercussions of the tournament reverberated around the globe in the weeks after the final.

Semi-final losers would play off in a 'Third Place' match at Wembley on Friday 22nd July; kicking off at 7:30 PM.

The Final would kick off at 3:00 PM on the following day, Saturday 23rd of July 1966.

Hang on, I hear you say, those matches are a tad close together! What about rest and recovery time for the players? What about getting the grounds and the pitches ready with hardly any turnaround?

If nothing else the congested fixture list for the 1966 tournament illustrates that when it comes to football the past really is a different country. Footballers – and spectators alike – just had to 'get on with it' in those days!

With the opening match scheduled to kick off at 7:30 PM on the evening of 4th July the whole tournament was scheduled to be done and dusted in twenty hectic days, with the four teams reaching the last four playing six matches in that time. Worse, once a team got to the knockout phases any match undecided at the ninety-minute, full-time mark would then be extended by another thirty minutes of 'extra time' to settle the issue.

There was no such thing as a penalty shootout in the 1966 World Cup. If two sides were still level at the conclusion of extra-time the winner was decided by the toss of a coin!

Understandably, the last thing any of the teams wanted was to be drawn in a 'group of death' right at the outset of the campaign.

The draw ceremony was attended by the Prime Minister and her husband, the Minister for Sport and Recreation and the Minister for London.

The actual draw was made by Susan Dexter, the wife of the Minister for Sport and Recreation, presumably to grace the otherwise somewhat downbeat event with a dash of glamour.

The most memorable quote from the occasion was from 'Mister Prime Minister' – a nickname both *The Daily Mirror* and *Tribune*, respectively the popular and the ideological mouthpieces of the Labour Party had attempted to pin to Colonel Francis St John Waters, VC, the day after he had married Margaret Thatcher, without any real success because the man was – apart from being marvellous copy – unremittingly honest about the fact that he was quote: 'Not the one wearing the trousers in this marriage!'

Everybody had taken to 'the Colonel'.

'Soccer's not really my game,' he freely confessed to all and sundry. 'I thought the offside law was tricky enough on the rugger field but these chaps make an absolute song and dance about it!'

Ever since the wedding the Colonel made a point of referring to his wife as 'Mrs T'.

When asked why he thought he had not been knighted yet he guffawed: 'I haven't done anything to warrant such an honour. I'm just a simple old soldier, don't you know!'

England were drawn in Group 1 with Spain, Chile and the weakest team in the tournament, Ghana. Scotland landed in a 'near death' combination in Group 2 with favourites Brazil, and Switzerland, always a redoubtable foe, and Mexico. Group 3 featured the South American heavyweights Argentina and Uruguay, Wales and Sweden. Group 4 pitted lightweights Northern Ireland and Colombia against Portugal who seemed to be Europe's answer to the Brazilians, and Italy, always a powerful World Cup force.

Eight grounds had been prepared to host the thirty-two matches of the FIFA World Cup of 1966: The Empire Stadium, to be renamed by Her Majesty the Queen the *Commonwealth Stadium* immediately prior to the opening game, at Wembley; Upton Park in East London; Hillsborough, the home of Sheffield Wednesday in Sheffield, and Villa Park, the ground of Aston Villa; Old Trafford, Manchester United's home; Leeds United's ground, Elland Road; and Middlesbrough's Ayresome Park; and Sunderland's Roker Park.

England's Group 1 would play its matches play at Wembley and Upton Park; Group 2 would be based at Sheffield and Birmingham; Group 3 at Manchester and Leeds; and Group 4 in the North East.

Quarter-Finals 1 to 4 would be played respectively at Wembley, Hillsborough, Villa Park and Roker Park (depending on whether England qualified as a group winner or runner up the venues for Quarter-Final 1 or 3 would be reversed so that England could play its match at Wembley).

A similar caveat applied to the venues for the Semifinals with one to be played at Wembley and the other at Villa Park.

The teams in Group 1, England, Chile, Spain and Ghana were the guests of the Army at Aldershot, Pirbright and Camberley in Surrey, taking over barracks and mess rooms emptied by troops serving in France. Accommodation was less of an issue for the teams in the other Groups where hotels re-opened to welcome the visitors and a clutch of country estates happily offered training grounds and facilities. Not that any of the nations involved in the 1966 World Cup could ever be in doubt, they could not help but be viscerally reminded every day, that they were in a country still recovering from a catastrophe beyond imagination.

They saw the sea of rubble that had been London; they were reassured that radiation levels were – in most places – the same as everywhere else in the world. But there were still 'no go' areas in the Thames estuary not a million miles from where two matches were to be played at Upton Park – the legacy of ground bursts at Chatham and Gravesend was to be to bar anybody not wearing full protective equipment for a generation coming within half-a-mile of the craters at ground zero – and elsewhere in the country there were blasted, dead zones for all that their hosts spoke optimistically about the 'greening' of the bombed areas.

The visitors got used to the chirping of radiation monitors in public places and were issued with 'dose meter badges' during their stay in England so that they could be confident that they were not being poisoned by the air their breathed.

A handful of players had stayed behind in South America; terrified by fears of returning irradiated. Fears unfounded if only because everywhere was as irradiated – well, more so – than it would have been without the war. That was the new condition of life on Earth and short of living in a lead box that was not going to change for tens, possibly hundreds of years.

Although the Jeremiads had predicted a ten or twenty or even fifty times higher long-term increase in background radiation as a result of the October War, by then the consensus was that levels were settling at between two to three times higher than pre-war. It was cold comfort because people who wanted to worry about it knew that the most pernicious fission products contributing to the raised background levels; Strontium-90, Iodine-131 and 133, had half-lives measured in tens of years.

Then as now it was generally accepted that humankind was embarking on a huge and potentially disastrous millennia-long physiological experiment living with what previously had been regarded as high *short-term* dosages of radiation, exposure to which would have permanently disqualified *any* worker in the nuclear industry from *ever* working with radioactive substances again.

In retrospect, the really surprising thing was that countries not directly touched by the recent war – Brazil, Uruguay and Argentina, and Ghana - had had the courage to send teams to England in the first place. Both Mexico and Colombia had experienced low levels of direct fallout from the immolation of Cuba by the USA, and the bombing of Galveston-Houston by the Soviets-Cubans.

Members of the Chilean team spoke about wanting to show solidarity with the English people when they landed in the British Isles, Pelé and many of his Brazilian teammates echoed those sentiments in later years. The plain truth is that it took great courage for all those from countries in the Americas to venture into what to them must have seemed like a 'danger zone'.

Of course, this was not appreciated at the time.

The British press treated 'Latin protests' about the way the draw was configured and what they viewed as the 'preference' that England were given in playing exclusively at Wembley as dire insults; not the complaints of men under great stress.

Brazil were the two times champions; everyone was looking to them to repeat their triumphs in Chile and Sweden in 1962 and 1958.

England were the host country; the hopes of the whole nation were unnaturally, perversely high and people too readily forget that wen Alf Ramsey was being overly dour, understated in everything he said and did he was desperately attempting to stop the media crushing his players under an intolerable weight of false expectation.

The other thing forgotten in all the kerfuffle of the weeks and the years to come was that Alf Ramsey was under no less pressure, than for example, the then twenty-eight-year old Antonio Ubaldo Rattín, the Boca Juniors midfielder whom destiny had determined should be the captain of Argentina.

Spare a thought for the young man who found himself leading his side to a land with which his country had recently been at war with; a country shamelessly inflamed by what he regarded as malicious, utterly unfounded lies about the way his countrymen had treated enemy soldiers and civilians in the re-conquest of Las Malvinas fifteen months before.

Even before they had kicked a ball in anger Rattin and his team mates were vilely abused. How on earth could he not have felt intimidated and angry? Rattin had good reason to suspect that his life would be forfeit if the soldiers and policemen guarding he and his team relaxed their guard for a moment, or frighteningly, simply stepped aside and allowed the mob to run riot.

How could the World Cup Finals in *England* ever be just about football for Antonio Rattin?

11 | Group 1 (London)

The opening match of the tournament had been scheduled for the evening of Monday 4th July because – you are not going to believe this - it was thought by the Organising Committee that this would reduce the crowd by half. If this sounds bizarre then John Joe Mears's World Cup 1966 Organising Committee was afraid that the newly re-established local transport infrastructure, the Army, Police and all the people staffing the great stadium could not guarantee the safety of the Queen and other VIPs and might not be able to cope if a capacity crowd turned up for the match.

There had been no 'trial run', and right up until the final days before the first match nobody had known if everything would be ready. Thus, the opening match of the tournament was in effect a massive operational test of the transportation systems bringing people into the otherwise wasted lands surrounding Wembley Park, the facilities of the stadium, the stewarding plan and so forth.

In the event well over a hundred thousand people packed into the new Commonwealth Stadium and thousands mingled outside eating and drinking the inadequately stocked tea and sandwich stalls dry and bare. Alcohol sales inside Wembley Park had been forbidden so there was little drunkenness.

At half-time an enterprising BBC man rigged speakers beneath the twin tower to broadcast the live radio commentary going out to the nation to the thousands milling along Wembley Way.

Mears's Organising Committee had correctly anticipated most of the logistics problems and others – like disruptions from gangs of pickpockets and the groups of people who refused to 'come in' from the surrounding ruins and regarded the 'intrusion' into their patch of devastation with hostility – and made, with the police and the military, sensible and for the time, oddly proportionate and detailed plans to deal with the most likely scenarios.

At this period bands of scavengers – some but not all criminal – still roamed the ruins although military interventions to take control of the old City, financial area, and successive amnesties had reduced the number of people 'living transient lives' in the former Greater London Area by an estimated three-quarters from its 1964 peak of about 100,000 in the previous twelve months.

Chaos was only ever a blink of an eye away.

Anybody flying over Wembley Park on the afternoon of the match would have imagined they were being treated to a bird's eye view of a giant refugee camp, some kind of British version of the displaced persons tented towns which had sprung up all over West Germany, Austria and Italy after the Second War.

There was nothing ad hoc, or 'it will be all right on the night' about the preparations.

Firstly, it was all part of a bigger plan to expand the existing, very large, Royal Engineer depots at Wembley and in the East End into major bases from which to organise and supply the next stage of the reconstruction of the Metropolis along the lines of Miriam Prior's vision of a 'Garden City' of hilltop villages.

Secondly, it was recognised early on that it would be impossible to bring in and transport out again, anywhere near the ninety-eight thousand five hundred people – the official capacity of the Commonwealth Stadium after it had been repaired, and its structure ruggedly reinforced – in any twenty-four-hour period. Theoretically, the rail lines had the capacity but in reality, probably not the rolling stock, carriages and the like and there simply were not sufficient buses to take the strain if there was a problem with the railway links.

The nearest undamaged, or rather, fully functioning towns were Slough fourteen miles to the west, and Watford (eight miles), Potters Bar (eleven miles) and Cheshunt (fifteen miles) to the north west, the north and the north east. The rail and road connections from Slough and Watford, and the roads down from Potters Bar and Cheshunt passed through mile upon mile of rubble fields to reach, sometimes very circuitously Wembley Park, a safe haven, an island of civilization. There was no question of allowing individuals or small groups of spectators to 'make their own way' to the matches held at the Commonwealth Stadium, although in the coming days and weeks probably thousands trekked through the wreckage, clogging the dusty sides of roads or picking their way through the shattered streets of north-west London.

In any event there were tents and camp beds, or palliases on the ground under canvas for as many as fifteen thousand people in Wembley Park and an Army soup kitchen equipped to feed as many mouths. There was piped potable water, a dozen big washrooms, and rank upon rank of latrines and the Park was supervised by some fifteen hundred officers and men of the joint, Army, Navy and RAF 'Task Force Wembley', supported by almost as many civilian, or auxiliary volunteer helpers.

Similar, albeit much smaller 'task forces' had been allocated to all of the venues although, in the event, at most of the non-London grounds the Football Association and the individual ground authorities obstructed the provision of 'free services', especially food which otherwise they would have profited from, and sometimes insisted that their own, local stewards took over from the Army and the Police inside and in the immediate environs of grounds contrary to the best efforts of the Organising Committee.

Other than at the entrance to Wembley Way, and guarding the stadium itself and visiting VIPs very few of the men in uniform were armed. That again, was a calculated decision taken to inculcate a relaxed atmosphere around the whole Park; although nearby, mainly out of sight – shielded from view by several small 'rubble hillocks' - a heavily armed detachment drawn from men of the Parachute Regiment stood ready in case of trouble less than a quarter of a mile from the twin towers.

Situated on recently cleared land to the east of the stadium a mobile hospital had been set up to deal with the inevitable accidents and mishaps that were likely to attend any event visited by tens of thousands of people, fully staffed by Royal Army Medical Corps personnel and the Surgeon Lieutenant-Commanders of the two frigates moored in the Thames below Tower Bridge for the duration of the tournament.

The 'arrangements' were tested very nearly to the point of destruction that night in July. The weather had been balmy that summer but a threat of thunder and lightning hung over Wembley Park, with dark clouds forcing the authorities to switch on the flood lights – one facility which had been fully tested – at around seven o'clock when the Sea King helicopter carrying the Queen, Prince Philip, the Prime Minister and her husband, and the Minister of Sport and his former Hardy Amies model wife, escorted by two Westland Wessex 'gunships' flew in from Windsor, some fifteen miles away.

The plan had been for Her Majesty and her party to disembark outside of the stadium will all due ceremony in the shadow of the famous twin towers; but the crowd had already spilled across the designated landing area by then.

No matter, there was a great big landing field inside the soon to be renamed Commonwealth Stadium so the Queen's noisy aerial carriage put down squarely in the centre circle of the pitch. The turf having been freshly watered, its wheels sank in several inches as it rolled to a halt, and the cabin steps cut further 'grooves' in the immaculate sward of the field of play.

The 'Football Association Three' – Sir Stanley Rous, John Joe Mears, and Harold Thompson – marched out to welcome their guests of honour, forming a line behind Miriam Prior and Major General David Willison, the incomparable Royal Engineer who had made it all possible.

The film crew who had set up to capture the Queen's arrival outside tried and failed to run into the stadium to record this somewhat low-key, no-nonsense scene; only to be thwarted by a cordon of scowling, suspicious-eyed men of the Black Watch to whom the honour and glory of protecting their monarch was not to be compromised by the requirements of a mere 'film crew' whom ought, they decided, to have been paying more attention when the Queen's Flight landed in a different place.

The Royal arrival was in any event recorded for posterity by the BBC cameras in the stands and by the pitch-side. The Corporation was to be criticised for its limited coverage of the tournament in later years; at the time it elected to concentrate all its resources on beaming live coverage – the first such sporting broadcast since the war – of all of England's matches from Wembley. Subsequently, it also decided to cover both the semi-finals, and the third-place play-off match on the night before the final. People tend to forget that the BBC was still a shadow of its pre-war self, and because of this the Organising Committee had invited British Pathé and others, including the surviving regional ITV – Independent Television – companies to cover additional matches in their own regions.

Whereas, today every minute of every match would be recorded from countless angles and perspectives; back in 1966 it was a minor miracle that fifteen of the thirty-two matches were broadcast or filmed in full, and that some cinematic record survives of all but five of the fixtures.

In England radio was still ubiquitous and in addition to the England matches full commentary was broadcast of fourteen others.

The cameras fully documented the extraordinarily good-natured chaos at Wembley on the opening night of the tournament. Officially, there were ninety-eight thousand five hundred people inside the old Empire Stadium when, before being presented to the English and Chilean elevens Her Majesty the Queen unveiled the plaque in the Royal Box renaming the great edifice the 'Commonwealth Stadium'.

Jimmy Armfield, the Blackpool full back had been named England captain when the squad was announced but had been doubtful for the Chile match right up until the weekend on account of a niggling calf strain. Had he been unfit Bobby Charlton would have been the man introducing the Queen and her party to the members of the team Alf Ramsey had selected to kick off England's quest for the Jules Rimet Trophy.

Ramsey had opted for caution, solidity and character.

Gordon Banks was in goal; no surprise there!

The back four comprised Armfield and Don Howe on the flanks, with Jack Charlton and Peter Swan in the middle. The selection of the elder Charlton, a giraffe like presence who could be counted on to snuff out most aerial threats, gave rise to discussion in the press box but not that of Peter Swan, whom it was known that Ramsey regarded as the best central defender in England.

In midfield Bobby Charlton was flanked by Nobby Stiles and Ron Flowers, the latter another veteran of the Chilean campaign four years before.

The front three were Terry Paine on the wing, and John Connelly and Derek Kevan.

The problem was, Bobby Charlton apart – Flowers form had been patchy in the practice matches – it was hard to see how the 'front men' were ever going to get the ball.

And so, in the way of these things, it went for much of the match, a drab, frustrating affair given extra, grim frissance by the goal gifted to the visitors in the sixth minute by a rare Peter Swan miss-header that fell obligingly at the feet of Chile's Rubén Marcos a couple of feet to the left of the penalty spot. Hardly believing his luck the twenty-three-year old snatched at the shot, scuffed the ball and sent it trickling and bobbling past Gordon Bank's despairing left hand into the very corner of the net.

Thereafter, the visitors dug in behind an eleven-man defence and allowed wave after wave of England attacks to break on what, until the final minutes of the match seemed like impregnable footballing earthworks.

Bobby Charlton and John Connelly tested the Chilean goalkeeper Juan Olivares from long-range and early in the second half both Connelly and Derek Kevan blasted wide from inside the penalty area. To their credit Ramsey's men did not wilt, shoulders did not sag and they kept pushing forward but by the time a speculative cross from Terry Paine was headed behind for an English corner in the eighty-sixth minute, all hope seemed lost.

Wembley erupted in a spontaneous, near hysterical uproar of relief and joy as Jack Charlton fought his way through a press of bodies – English and Chilean – to rise high above the six-yard line and head the ball bullet-like at, and a moment later, through Olivares's hands to equalise.

England might have stolen an unlikely victory with the last kick of the match but Derek Kevan's lunging contact with a cross deflected off a defender's shin and rolled agonisingly wide of goal with the Chilean goalkeeper completely wrong-footed.

Nevertheless, England had obeyed the first rule of all tournaments: whatever you do, do not lose the first game! Never mind that even in defence Chile had looked the more accomplished technical side, their players more comfortable on the ball and England's lions by comparison a little leaden-footed and predictable.

Two days later Spain thrashed new boys Ghana six-nil. The Ghanaians had put up a brave fight for forty minutes; then the flood gates had opened and the Spaniards playing with no little flair and élan, not to mention clinical accuracy had strolled to a victory every bit as easy as the eventual score line indicated. The biggest surprise of the night was that over twenty-three thousand people had filed into the Commonwealth Stadium to watch the match.

Many of these dedicated souls had probably never gone home after the England-Chile encounter. Ticket prices varied up and down the land; at Wembley and the two matches in East London at Upton Park standing on the terraces was free, with a seat in the stands varying from a few pennies to a maximum of one-pound sterling. Given that public transport was heavily subsidised or free in that era, and that all the services in the tented camp at Wembley Park and its smaller analogue at Poplar were supplied gratis to anybody foolhardy, brave or dedicated enough to venture into the bombed city, the World Cup of 1966 was never going to be any kind of money-spinner. Visiting teams were paid their legitimate costs in full directly from the Government exchequer and the Football Association took its meagre cut of the gate receipts at the other – non-London – grounds without complaint.

Truly, the past is another country...

Two days later at Upton Park in front of 21,078 spectators – perhaps two thirds of the capacity of the patched-up Boleyn Road ground – Chile rifled another four goals past the Ghanaians without reply, and briefly, were alone at the top of Group 1.

The crunch game of the Group was undoubtedly that between England and Spain on the afternoon of Saturday 9th July. This time the authorities avoided the chaos of the previous Monday. A limit had been put on how many people would be allowed into the Wembley Park 'district' and orderly queues formed outside the stadium several hours before kick-off. Many people were refused entrance; there would be no repeat of the dangerous over-crowding of the opening match and this time a more realistic attendance figure of 96,156 persons was recorded. Notwithstanding, many who were present that day claim the real figure might have been 105,000 or more!

Jimmy Armfield had had to sit out this match. Alf Ramsey had reacted by switching Nobby Stiles into the back four and bringing in Blackburn Rover's Keith Newton. This raised a lot of eyebrows; the side looked unbalanced with too many men playing out of position, although nobody objected to Bobby Charlton being left pulling the strings in the middle of the park with a licence to maraud forward at will.

Both Newton and Stiles cleared off the line in the first thirty minutes as the Spaniards gave their hosts a footballing lesson. England chased the ball like carthorses trying to catch hares. It was a miracle that Ramsey's men only trailed to a single close-range strike from *El Brujo* – 'the Wizard' – Real Madrid's twenty-six-year old outside right Amancio Amaro Varela.

Football, as we all know, is a game of two halves and this contest was a classic example. It was as if the Spanish having exhausted their portfolio of tricks, had run themselves into the ground and within minutes of the restart John Connelly had wrestled a cross from Bobby Charlton into the net. Thereafter, an unrelenting siege of the Spanish goal commenced. Inevitably, Derek Kevan headed home the winner in the seventy-fourth minute after he and Connelly had missed a dozen chances to put the result beyond doubt.

Problematically, in scoring Kevan fell awkwardly and was a passenger for the last quarter-of-an-hour of the match with the shoulder injury that was going to rule him out of the rest of the competition and effectively end his professional career.

Given that England's only remaining fixture was against the game but outclassed Ghanaians the pressure was off, barring something utterly extraordinary – Spain or Chile winning their contest by a dozen goals – Ramsey's men would surely beat Ghana and go forward as top dog in Group 1.

England's footballers suddenly discovered that they were national heroes on a par with any of the men who had won Victoria Crosses in the battles of the Mediterranean and the Persian Gulf in 1964.

'We had only actually won one game,' Bobby Charlton recollected. 'We could easily have lost them both our first two games. Alf was right when he said we ought to take everything we read in the papers with a pinch of salt.'

Undeniably, the nation had needed one sort of hero in 1964 and another altogether now; and the England football team were IT!

On the evening of Tuesday 12th July England walked out in front of a crowd of 88,744 and after twenty frustrating minutes of hammering at the gates of a brave, ultimately futile Ghanaian defence ran out the winners nine-nil.

Alf Ramsey had re-instated the fit again Jimmy Armfield for Keith Newton and Southampton's Geoff Hurst had come in for the injured Derek Kevan. He had also 'rested' Ken Flowers in favour of Huddersfield Town's twenty-three-year old Michael O'Grady in midfield; and swapped Alan Ball, Blackpool's live-wire twenty-one-year old winger for the more experienced, steadier Terry Paine.

The match is now remembered for the six goals scored by Geoff Hurst, four of them headers – three making contact with balls clipped into the near post at pace by O'Grady – and by the fact it was the only time both Charlton brothers scored in the same match for England. By then John Connelly's clinical side-foot into the net past the onrushing goalkeeper – who rugby-tackled him as the ball rolled into the net – was long-forgotten.

These days Ghana would have finished the match with five or six players; their goalie's enthusiastic misdemeanour being only one of a catalogue of mistimed and middlingly brutal assaults – to their credit mainly 'on the ball' – during the match, after which several England players were left nursing a miscellany of painful 'lumps and bumps'.

Football is – although one might not know it now – a game of physical contact. Most players drew the line at kicking 'lumps' out of an opponent 'off the ball' but if the ball was anywhere near most things were, as in love and war, considered fair.

Spain beat Chile three-one in East London the next day to finish second in Group 1.

GROUP 1	P.	W.	D.	L.	For	Ag.	Pts.
England	3	2	1	0	12	2	5
Spain	3	2	0	1	10	3	4
Chile	3	1	1	1	6	4	3
Ghana	3	0	0	3	0	19	0

Immediately, all eyes turned to the last match in Group 2 to decide whom England would face in the quarter-finals at Wembley the coming Saturday. The Brazilians had brushed aside Mexico four-one while England had been making hay at Wembley; so that meant everything hung on Scotland's fixture with Switzerland at Villa Park the next day.

12 | Group 2 (Hillsborough & Villa Park)

Brazil were to football what Don Bradman's Australians had been to cricket twenty years before. They were invincibles, untouchables, without peers. For all that several stalwarts of their 1958 and 1962 World Cup winning sides were getting a little long in the tooth; Pelé was in his prime and nobody doubted the brilliance of the next crop of outlandishly gifted youngsters clinging to the great man's coat tails.

Captained by their brick wall of a central defender thirty-six-year old Hilderaldo Luiz Bellini and led towards goal by twenty-five-year old Edson Arantes do Nascimento – known to the world at large as Pelé, the Brazilians also boasted, looking to end their international careers in one more blaze of glory thirty-three-year old Santos midfield legend Zito (José Ely de Miranda) and Botafogo's thirty-two-year old free-scoring forward Manuel Francisco dos Santos, the legendary Garrincha ('little bird'). The younger generation included sixteen-year-old Edu, Jonas Eduardo Américo destined to become a Santos and Brazil footballing institution; twenty-five-year old master midfield general Gérson de Oliveira Nunes; twenty-one-year old all-time great Jair Ventura Filho, famously better known as Jairzinho, and the likes of nineteen-year old Cruzeiro's free-scoring forward Eduardo Gonçalves de Andrade (Tostão). And these men were just the headline acts in a squad packed with quick, hard-tackling defenders, wily, twinkle-footed midfielders who seemed to have been born with a chess player's understanding of the three-dimensional opportunities presented by a football field, and a clutch of lethally prolific goal-scorers.

Brazil were not unbeatable; it was just that hardly anybody had beaten them for years. Oddly, although England had only played the Brazilians four times - between 1956 and 1962 under Walter Winterbottom's stewardship – they had a respectable record against the World Cup Champions. England had beaten Brazil four-two at Wembley in 1956 and held the eventual winners goalless in the 1958 World Cup, before losing a friendly in Brazil two-nil, and that Quarter-Final in Chile four years ago. Not that any of this was any help to Scotland, who had never played Brazil, or the other two teams in Group 2, Mexico and Switzerland.

Switzerland, like England had not played an international, or even practice matches for over three years until that spring. Their squad numbered only seventeen, several of those named in the first 'short list' in Geneva having later been discovered to have died or disappeared, or simply elected not to travel abroad.

On the evening of Wednesday 5th July Brazil outclassed, bamboozled and toyed with the labouring Swiss at the Hillsborough ground of Sheffield Wednesday in front of 33,943 mainly neutral supporters who had come along, to a man and a boy, to witness the South American magic of Pelé, Garrincha and company. Pelé did not disappoint, scoring two goals, Zita another and Tostão walking a fourth into the net after Garrincha and Jairzinho had ripped the exasperated Swiss defence to shreds.

The next day in Birmingham in front of a capacity 46,412 crowd at Villa Park Scotland huffed and puffed and utterly failed to blow down the Mexicans. Mexico actually created the clearer cut chances in a dull, bad-tempered match in which two players from each side were booked; not for kicking lumps out of each other but for arguing with the referee.

Two days later Scotland found themselves – courtesy of the ludicrously condensed schedule – walking out at Hillsborough to face the rampant Brazilians. Lucky to be only a goal down at half-time they rallied famously in the second period. Denis Law equalised only for those granite gateposts in the heart of the Scottish defence – Billy McNeill and John Greig – to be left as helpless witnesses to a brilliant six pass move which allowed Pelé to deftly lift the ball over Kilmarnock goalie Campbell Forsyth to put the Brazilians back in the driving seat.

The next twenty minutes have gone down in Scottish footballing folklore; with time running out Jimmy Johnstone ripped in a series of crosses, Jim Baxter began to weave spells in the Brazilian half, Denis Law missed one, then another half-chance until finally in the eighty-eighth minute Alan Gilzean, the Dundee centre forward who was only playing because Manchester United's David

Herd had not recovered from a dead leg suffered against Mexico two days ago, crouched low to head the goal that saved Scotland's World Cup.

For another day at least.

The next night Mexico and Switzerland cancelled each other out, drawing 1-1. With a match to play Brazil looked the likeliest to top the Group but mathematically all four teams still had a chance of going through to the quarter-finals.

Needless to say, the Brazilians tore the Mexican defence apart in exactly the way Scotland had not on Wednesday 12th July at Hillsborough in front of over thirty-three thousand mesmerised fans; in a performance so complete that when the Mexicans reduced the final margin to 1-4 with an improbable late goal nobody really believed their eyes at first.

Garrincha, Jairzinho (two) and Pelé had scored goals of subtlety and in the case of Jairzinho's second, of spectacular power from the edge of the penalty area.

At Villa Park on the 13th July Scotland's task was simple. All Jock Stein's men had to do was avoid defeat and they would be guaranteed a quarter-final showdown, probably with England at Wembley that coming weekend. However, as any sportsman will tell one, knowing what one 'has to do' is often a decidedly mixed blessing.

Matters were complicated because although David Herd was fit, Denis Law was afflicted by what was politely described as 'a stomach upset' on the night before the match and was still, violently by some accounts, ill the next morning. Gilzean, the hero of Hillsborough, therefore remained in the team. This was hardly ideal as he and Herd, although different types of player liked to occupy the same space, make the same kinds of runs and haunt the same quarters of the opposition penalty area. Another absentee was Jimmy Johnstone, nursing a sprained ankle still swollen from the Brazil game, so in came Dundee's Charlie Cooke, yet another off the endless production line of Scots with mesmeric feet.

It was a mistake by Cooke that allowed René-Pierre Quentin to run onto a wayward pass into a one-on-one with Campbell Forsyth before John Greig clipped his heels and gave away a penalty, which Vittore "Vito" Gottardi duly thumped into the space Campbell Forsyth had just vacated as he speculatively – guessing wrongly - threw himself to his left.

The crowd, listed as 43,125, fell deathly silent.

Jock Stein was not the sort of manager who minced words.

In the second half Scotland emerged with Alan Gilzean playing on the left-hand side up front and David Herd usually a few paces behind him sticking to the right of the field; suddenly there was space between the two men as the Swiss peeled off and man marked each striker. Whereas in the first half they had bottled up the two predators by occupying the areas of the pitch that they both wanted to operate in, and were in fact competing for, now the Scots were able to move the Swiss defenders around and break up their previously disciplined defence in depth.

On the hour David Herd snapped in a shot from the right-centre of the goal from about twenty yards that threatened to break the crossbar, Alan Gilzean threw himself at the rebound and in a flurry of feet and the goalkeeper's flapping hands nudged the ball home for the equaliser.

Charlie Cooke's turn to reel off his party pieces; he danced past two defenders five minutes later and passed the ball into the Swiss net. Switzerland were beaten by then; run into the ground and a little dispirited, knowing that their gallant against the odds journey to England had been for nought.

GROUP 2	P.	W.	D.	L.	For	Ag.	Pts.
Brazil	3	2	1	0	10	4	5
Scotland	3	1	2	0	4	3	4
Mexico	3	0	2	1	2	5	2
Switzerland	3	0	1	2	3	7	1

England would play Scotland at Wembley on

Saturday 16th July in Quarter-Final No. 1. Much as this might be Scotland's dream tie, it was not Jock Stein's.

Brazil, meanwhile would play Spain in the next round in Quarter-Final No. 3

If Jock Stein might not be celebrating Alf Ramsey must have been sighing and huge sigh of relief. Brazil, England's nemesis in Chile four years before had been avoided, consigned to the other half of the knock out draw; therefore, if England got past Scotland, they would not have to face the current champions until the Final.

Of course, England had to get there first...

13 | Group 3 (Elland Road & Old Trafford)

'Group of death' was not a commonly used footballing phrase back in 1966 but had it been, Group 3 would have qualified. Argentina was probably the strongest team but the others were almost as good most days and now and then every bit as good as the men from Buenos Aires.

But and there is always a big 'but' about comparing the teams in England that summer. There was no reliable competitive yardstick by which to judge any of the European teams. For example, Sweden had impressed in two tours of Scotland and England that year winning as many games as they lost playing 'friendlies' against top club sides *but* how would that apparent good form actually translate into tournament football?

Sweden had, like its Scandinavian neighbours Norway and Denmark been in the firing line – most likely – inadvertently, accidentally, in the October War. None of its major cities had been directly targeted but near misses and fallout had brought the country to its knees in 1963. In 1964 the Swedes had concluded a mutual support pact with Norway and Denmark – both of which had been much more heavily damaged and suffered twenty to thirty percent population losses - under which the three countries instituted the freedom of movement of goods and people across their share boundaries and waters, and promoted the rejuvenation of economic, cultural and sporting links. Although the latter had mainly been in areas of traditional Nordic sports, a triangular annual football tournament had been held in the spring of 1964 and 1965, won conclusively by Sweden both times and Scottish 'Football League' representative elevens had visited Malmo and Stockholm in May 1964 and then again in 1965.

At the time of the 1966 World Cup in England the worst kept secret in England was that the Nordic Alliance had formally sought associate membership of the CMAFTA – the Commonwealth Mutual Assistance and Free Trade Agreement organisation at the heart of the New Commonwealth fashioned out of the aftermath of the October War – and that Margaret Thatcher was going to strongly support bringing the Scandinavian 'three' onboard at the forthcoming second annual CMAFTA conference due to be held in Ottawa in August of that year.

Everywhere in England that the Swedish team went, every time they stepped onto a football pitch they were greeted as if they were on home turf. The Swedes had been through what the British had gone through; they had refused to lie down, to give in and now they were 'in it with us'. So, although on paper they were not the strongest team in Group 3 playing against them could be like playing against twelve, not eleven men.

There were those – a minority, admittedly - who suggested that Wales might be black horses in the tournament. Always somewhat in the shadow of England and Scotland in the British Isles the recent war had been a cruel equaliser, barely touching Wales's relatively small, but talented pool of international class players.

They had lost their talisman, John Charles to sickness in the winter of 1962-63, like so many others he had disappeared in the post-war mayhem but in Wyn Davies, who plied his trade with Bolton Wanderers, and his namesake, Ron, Luton Town's prolific goal-scorer, Wales had real menace in attack, and like Blackburn Rovers' central defender Mike England would probably have walked into Alf Ramsey's squad. The three men were all in their twenty-fifth years. Wyn Davies had already earned the sobriquet 'Wyn the Leap', and he, Ron Davies and Mike England were all touted to be snapped up by wealthier clubs as soon as the post-war restrictions on registration – a thinly-veiled restraint on the movement of players between clubs – was lifted, a thing mooted for the end of the coming 1966-67 season. In fact, under threat of a players strike and legal action by the Professional Footballers Association – reformed only on 1st January 1966, the Football League in effect, reverted to the regulations relating to transfers in effect on the day before the October War on 1st August 1966.

Wyn and Ron Davies were keeping Newcastle United's Ivor Allchurch, a stalwart of the side since the early 1950s on the side lines. Now thirty-six, he remained a fit, industrious, intelligent inside forward if not the prolific striker he had been in his pomp.

Rightly, many in Wales still regard the mid- to late-sixties as being a mini-golden age.

A generation of young players was coming through, thriving on the adversity of the era. Beside Mike England in defence there was Birmingham City's Terry Hennessey and Cardiff City's Peter Rodrigues, aged twenty-three and twenty-two respectively, and on the wing another twenty-two-year old, Ronnie Rees. Even in goal there was fierce competition: in the summer of 1966 it was nip and tuck whether twenty-three-year old West Bromwich Albion keeper Tony Millington, or Leeds United's Gary Sprake, two years his junior would stand between the posts in the World Cup. Of the two Sprake was the more fallible; as befitted one of the best 'shot stoppers' in the game he was wont, inevitably, to occasionally err.

It was Millington – ironically, the safer pair of hands - who got the nod for Wales in the crunch match of Group 3 against Group favourites Argentina and it was his momentary fumble, under extreme pressure, which ultimately divided the sides in a match dominated by the Welsh for long periods.

But more of that below!

Football in the Argentine was to come to seem like a blood sport to English and Scottish teams in the coming years; but that is to do a fundamental injustice to the technique and artfulness of the marvellous players who graced its stage in the sixties. Domestically, Argentina's domestic football had the grace and the brutality of the bull ring, and a savage, compelling finesse and ruthlessness played out before baying crowds of ecstatic supporters in sun-burned, dusty concrete stadia in the heat of the day. It was an environment which bred hard men, proud men and often when the Argentine sent its favourite sons abroad, they felt themselves to be totally, and unjustly misunderstood.

Uruguay, the second South American team drawn in Group 3 was alike, and yet completely unalike its geographical near neighbour. Separated by the River Plate and a divergent history; its teams had a similar solidarity, a similar 'thou shalt not pass' mentality with a preference for picking defenders with 'legs like tree trunks', but in that age, less artistry. Whereas Argentina fielded elevens that might – but for their inbuilt negativity away from home – have been more than just shadows of the great Brazilian sides, Uruguay was, despite its magnificent record in past World Cup Finals, at the beginning of a decade in the doldrums of international football.

Nobody seriously expected a riot of attacking football from Group 3; and nobody was disappointed. For the aficionados there were several fascinating tactical duels, true footballing 'arm-wrestles' punctuated with shameless cynicism and violence played in a frankly, appalling spirit and only at the very end when there was nothing left to play for except honour, a single free-flowing contest played out between sportsman a little ashamed of what had gone before.

On Tuesday 5th July Argentina kicked Sweden out of the World Cup. Literally, the Swedes were kicked this way, that way, and every which way with four of the men who played in that dreadful exhibition at Old Trafford that night missing both of the following Group games. It was one of those matches where the 'tackles started at waist high' and carried on getting higher as the match went on! The referee, a dapper Mexican, Senior Rudolfo Matthias who had seen this sort of thuggery a lot in his travels around South America had, by and large, turned a blind eye although he had at one point booked the Swedish Captain, Tore Klas Agne Simonsson, for protesting after he had been kicked – on the ground – for the second time. Had Argentina come to Manchester to play football they might have run in half-a-dozen goals in the second half as Sweden's walking wounded limped and staggered hither and thither.

Remarkably, having presided over this carnage Senior Matthias was later rewarded by being given the honour to referee one of the quarter-finals!

The next evening Wales got a dose of the same treatment from the Uruguayans at Elland Road, Leeds. However, unlike the Swedes the Welsh gave as good as they got, cheered on by a vociferously partisan crowd of 34,003 mainly very angry men hailing from the distant valleys of their homeland. However, even when the Uruguayan Captain, Horacio Troche Herrera, was sent off for punching – well, attempting to punch – Mike England to the floor mid-way through the second-half, Wales could find no way past the forest of immovable defenders barring their way to goal.

It should be noted, and emphasised that Mike England was six feet two inches tall and built like a heavyweight boxer in training and although momentarily put down on one knee there was never any prospect of him going down for the count. In fact, had not two of his team mates jumped on him his assailant would have been even sorry than, in the event, he was.

Somewhat bruised and already a point adrift of Argentina, Wales moved on to Manchester to confront the 'animals' who had, with impunity, waged 'footballing war' on the unfortunate Swedes two nights before. There might have been a dozen, or a score of incredibly brave Argentine supporters in the 31,906 people in the crowd that night but certainly no more than that!

In the furore of the Argentina-Sweden game the sporting press had almost but not completely forgotten about England's less than impressive performance against Chile; and in the way of newspapers down the ages were treating the Argentine campaign in England as an extension of 'unfinished business' in the South Atlantic in ways that were every bit as shameless as some of the Argentine team's tactics on the field.

So, in the hands of forty-one-year old optician, referee Hector Benes, a native of Lisbon, Portugal the 'battle of Old Trafford' commenced in an atmosphere that would have been familiar to any man or woman who had queued to get into the Colosseum to watch any of the repeat matches between the Christians and the lions in olden times.

To everybody's surprise the Argentines played neat, precise football mostly in the Welsh half for twenty-five minutes, testing Tony Millington three or four times before *Wyn the Leap* Davies thudded a header against the left-hand post of goalkeeper Antonio Roma. Roma, who had played for Boca Juniors since 1960 was known as 'Tarzan' in Argentina because of the extravagantly reckless way he hurled himself about his goal mouth. After this first scare, he heaped scorn on the men in front of him and gesticulated angrily, and when five minutes later he barely managed to scramble a low shot from Ronnie Rees around the same post Wyn Davies had tested, he was incandescent.

To say that the 'shutters came down' would be an understatement. Leaving a single man up front, fleet-footed nineteen-year old River Plate striker Oscar Más, the South Americans pulled everybody back behind the ball and thereafter, the 'unpleasantness' was not long-delayed.

The first man to feel the pain was Ron Davies, hacked down by Roberto Oscar Ferreiro and then 'accidentally' stamped on by at least one other defender. Referee Hector Benes probably did not believe what he had just witnessed; otherwise he must have at least booked *somebody.* Unfortunately, he booked nobody and meekly endured a verbal tirade from Argentine Captain Antonio Rattin for allowing the game to be halted so long while Davies was receiving treatment on the ground.

Many Welshmen swear that they still bear the scars of that day, albeit with pride. 'It was being spat at that was the worst', one veteran recollected decades later. "Everything else was well, bearable but at home we never spat at each other. Yes, we'd take a swing at somebody if we lost our rag but we'd never kick a man when he was down. To be honest the only reason we didn't retaliate, well not that much, anyway, was because none of us had been brought up to behave that way on a football pitch...'

In fact, Wales had four or five half-chances to snatch the match in the second half and took none of them, Argentina got a single sniff at the Wales goal and that was that. Alfredo *'El Tanque'* Rojas ran at the Welsh defence from the centre circle and from around thirty yards out struck a shot that bounced in front of the diving Tony Millington. The ball half-rebounded off the goalkeeper's chest and as he struggled to regain his feet Oscar Más gleefully swooped on the bobbling ball and buried it in the back of the net.

Sweden's World Cup hopes were extinguished the following evening in Leeds in front of a sympathetic crowd of 19,408 – remarkably, the lowest gate of any match in the finals – by a single goal scored three minutes into the second-half by possibly the best player on the field, twenty-three-year old Peñarol playmaker and striker Pedro Rocha whose personal reputation was to flower in the years leading up to and immediately after the Mexico

World Cup on 1970. His passing, ball-carrying and general marshalling of the Uruguayan midfield that evening against what was almost a second string Swedish side was a sign of things to come.

Confident expectations of a bloodbath at Elland Road where Argentina and Uruguay squared up to determine which side should head the group came to nothing. The two Latin American rivals played out the tamest of tame goalless draws in front of 24,702 disappointed spectators who had – to a man - paid good money to see a gladiatorial slaughterhouse. In a match played as if it were a contactless exhibition there were rare attacks, many intricate and ultimately unrewarded passing movements, and several players rolled out training ground trick shots and minor marvels of uncontested ball control.

The crowd chanted 'FIX! FIX! FIX!'

There may or may not have been a tacit, unwritten agreement between the sides to 'shut out' Wales; but most football historians simply accept that it was in both teams' best interests not to incur injuries to key players, or to risk their existing positions as first and second in Group 3.

The reasons why hardly mattered because by the time Wales and Sweden faced off at Old Trafford neither could qualify for the knock out stages of the tournament.

In front of 30,852 people the sides attacked from start to finish. Wales were the better, more penetrative side; Sweden were immensely game, refusing to admit defeat until the final whistle.

Two Wyn Davies first-half headers and a scorching second-half strike from Ron Davies, countered by goals in each period by thirty-two-year old Henry Larsson – only playing because Sweden's other strikers were all injured – playing in his third and last game for his country, kept the crowd on its toes until the death in a match subsequently touted as one of the most entertaining of the entire tournament.

GROUP 3	P.	W.	D.	L.	For	Ag.	Pts.
Argentina	3	2	1	0	2	0	5

Uruguay	3	1	2	0	1	0	4
Wales	3	1	1	1	3	3	3
Sweden	3	0	0	3	2	5	0

It would be no exaggeration that the news Argentina were – as Group 3 winners – now in England and Scotland's half of the knock out draw, and might conceivably meet either in the Semi-Final, was quite sufficient to make the great men of the Football Association, not to mention many in the corridors of power in Oxford, choke on their breakfasts the next morning.

Politics and sport are not, and have never been, separate. Just as diplomacy is war by other means, so sport is winning influence and assuaging, or inflaming, hearts and minds without actually resorting to armed conflict. Better to settle tribal squabbles by bat or ball, boot or athletic exploit than by outright warfare.

Problematically, given the state of the post-October War world sport had endless scope for starting, not ending the troubles of nations.

14 | Group 4 (Ayresome & Roker Park)

What of referees and sporting officialdom? If the tournament in England changed one thing for the better it was probably that it prompted the authorities to begin the long, painful process that, by trial and error, by which national and international associations – including FIFA in its reconstituted incarnation ahead of the 1970 tournament - abandoned an essentially laisse faire attitude to what went on in matches and became pro-actively involved in improving, then controlling conduct on the field and eradicating the worst excesses witnessed in England forever.

However, in England in 1966 *most* of the referees and linesmen officiating in *most* of the matches concerned themselves with blowing up for obvious fouls, watching the offside line, awarding goals and keeping time. To a man they took exception to dissent and the myriad of other forms of disrespect towards them and their dignity and at least two of the five sendings-off and perhaps fifty percent of all bookings were for showing dissent or committing acts of unsportsmanlike conduct (that is, being rude to the referee).

Few referees thought it was their job to protect the footballers *in their care*, several of whom suffered career-threatening or ending injuries as a result of blatant foul play in the course of the tournament's thirty-two matches. If one was to apply modern day standards of officiating professional football matches one might consider that the officials, by any rational standard, lost control of many of the games in 1966. Applying those same standards clearly, only a minority of those 1966 officials were remotely up to the job; many were unfit, either physically or temperamentally and some – probably, judging by the decisions they gave – had a poor or negligible, or if one is being charitable, eccentric understanding of the laws of football.

Not that the standard of refereeing in England was uniformly 'top notch' at that time; just better than that which the world got to see displayed in the first major global sporting event of the post-cataclysm epoch.

In Group 4 three schools of European footballing culture and that of Colombia clashed; and the Italians, feeling themselves to be playing in a country that was in every way hostile to them adopted the 'Argentina model of qualification'. To be fair the Italians were markedly less gratuitously violent, their style was to niggle and nip at the opposition rather than to hack and kick at every opportunity and there was never remotely the animus between the Italian side and opposing elevens that there was between say, the Argentines and the Scots.

Portugal were far from the rank outsiders that they were painted before the tournament. The Portuguese had come a long way since they were beaten ten-nil in Lisbon by one of Walter Winterbottom's first England sides in 1947. Sporting Lisbon and Benfica had been among Europe's top clubs at the time of the October War, with Benfica the reigning European Champions having won the competition in 1961-62 for the second successive year, and the national eleven boasting talent gathered from all over the crumbling, yet still far flung Portuguese empire.

All in all, 'dark horses' better described the Portuguese. Over half the squad, comprising a mix of experience and youth sprinkled with players who would have strolled into any other side in the tournament, Brazil included, was from the two great Lisbon clubs and played from the outset with a confidence and a zest noticeably on short supply in most of the other group matches in 1966.

The Benfica contingent was led by thirty-year old Mozambique-born team captain Mário Esteves Coluna, a five-feet seven-and-a-half inch-tall barrel of fire who never stopped running and whose influence on the field belied his unprepossessing stature. For club and country twenty-two-year-old force of nature António Simões da Costa - or more commonly just 'Simões' to the Benfica faithful – played on Coluna's left. To the captain's right would always be twenty-nine-year old free-scoring winger José Augusto. Also, in the squad were Benfica stalwarts Fernando Cruz and José Torres, and the man who was to be the star of the World Cup Finals of 1966, and after Pelé the greatest footballer of the age, twenty-four-year old Eusébio da Silva Ferreira, better known to everybody who knows anything about association football as simply 'Eusébio'.

Eusébio was the fourth child of a white Angolan railway worker father and a black Portuguese Mozambican mother in Lourenco Marques and had been in Benfica's European Cup winning team of 1962. He was a formidable athlete, lighting fast and, if a little right-footed, deadly in front of goal on the ground or in the air. Throughout his career to date he had scored at or better than a goal per game at whatever level, club or international, domestic or European. To Portuguese fans he was already *O Rei* – the King, or the Black Pearl. After his exploits in England in 1966 he would forever be 'the *Black Panther*' to the world at large.

Thirty-four-year old Belenenses goalkeeper José Pereira had edged ahead of Sporting Lisbon's Joaquim Carvalho that spring; elsewhere Sporting's stars played side by side throughout the team with their great Benfica rivals.

The Portuguese found themselves walking out at one of the grimmest grounds in England, Middlesbrough's Ayresome Park in front of 27,791 spectators on a cool Teesside evening in North Yorkshire against a slick rather than penetrative Colombian side even less acclimatised to the English North East than they were!

More than any other, Group 4 was played out in an undamaged industrial landscape by teams accommodated in some of the most spectacularly beautiful locations in the country. This contrast between the forever bleak majesty of the land outside the old powerhouses of the first industrial revolution, towns – Middlesbrough and Sunderland – still wedded to the steel and shipbuilding industries upon which their former wealth had been founded, stayed with all the visitors long after they departed England's fair and variously blasted land.

Ayresome Park and Roker Park were architectural children of the two great cities' heritage; great monolithic constructs, the one grim the other a huge partially roofed shed, both with tall terraces and very few amenities that were in any sense modern. Anybody visiting the ground in the 1930s would have recognised them instantly, for they were what they were, marvellous old footballing citadels and each the beating hearts of their city tribes.

Ayresome Park's occupants, Middlesbrough; and Roker Park's denizens, Sunderland had been in the doldrums, albeit fighting for promotion out of League Division 2 to the top flight of English football in the autumn of 1962. Both had automatically walked into the re-constituted First Division and finished the season recently completed in the upper half of the table; with both sets of fans somewhat aggrieved that only one of their heroes – Brian Clough – had made it into the England squad. Nonetheless, footballing folk in the North East would turn out in their droves to be a part of *England's* World Cup.

Portugal stuttered in the first-half against Colombia, with José Carlos, the twenty-four-year old Sporting centre-half uncharacteristically clattering into the back of striker Delio Gamboa to concede a thirtieth minute penalty kick which duly saw Portugal go in at half-time a goal down.

Once or twice in the first forty-five minutes Eusébio's lightning reflexes and sprinting power had panicked the Colombian defence. Almost before the crowd had settled after the start of the second half a back-peddling Colombian back four had allowed the Black Panther to fire in a piledriver that thumped into a post and ricocheted across the face of the goal into the path of José Augusto. With the scores levelled so quickly the Colombians' shoulders sagged and two more goals – by Simões and José Carlos, atoning for his earlier sin conceding the penalty - in ten minutes finished the game as a contest.

The following night Northern Ireland were taught a sanguinary lesson by the Italians at Roker Park in front of 38,118 on Wearside. The Italians allowed the Irish to roar forward, took the ball, kept it for long periods and during the course of the match fashioned three clear goal-scoring chances, taking two of them with clinical efficiency. The Ulstermen's problem was – the crowd decided fairly early in the proceedings – that they only had one big idea. Specifically, to give the ball to George Best and basically, see what happened next. It was not a wholly unreasonable plan; after all, it had worked many times for League Champions Manchester United in the season just finished. But of course, United had not come up against the Italian national side in any one of their fifty to sixty odd league and cup games in the season of 1965-66, and neither had George Best until that night in Sunderland.

Northern Ireland were not *just* twenty-year old George Best, any more than Pelé was Brazil, it was more that the Ulsterman did not have a Garrincha or a Jairzinho in their squad to back him up. Once, the 'Belfast Boy' very nearly dribbled all the way to the six-yard box before finally three Italian defenders closed him down; otherwise he was so frustrated that by the final quarter of the game he repeatedly passed the ball back to whoever had given it to him as if to say 'what do you expect me to do?'

The Irish had a number of quality players in their ranks, like twenty-seven-year-old Johnny Crossan, Brian Clough's striking partner at Sunderland. Alex Elder, the Burnley left back was a fixture in the side. Derek Dougan, the rugged twenty-eight-year old Aston Villa centre forward, oddly picked ahead of Johnny Crossan on his home ground, was among the best target men in the British Isles on his day, and there were few better goalkeeping prospects than Watford's twenty-one-year old Pat Jennings.

But there was only one George Best.

Anybody who had ever seen the kid play knew that!

The Italians had not come to England with high hopes, there participation having been in doubt practically right up to the moment the team left Rome to travel to England. As many as seven first choices for the eventual nineteen-man Italian squad had declined to travel, either to Rome or to England. Italy was a country on the verge of disintegration and all the men who came to England in 1966 must have kept one eye looking over their shoulder listening for news from home. So, not for the Italians the luxury of a slew of practice games or notions of dazzling English crowds with Roman sleight of hand or showing off. No, they were in England to progress as far as possible in the competition, to preserve Italian honour and given their limited preparation and resources, pragmatism was to be the key word in their campaign.

Stop George Best and Northern Ireland are half-beaten; that was the mantra at Roker Park and it worked beyond all the expectations of twenty-six-year old Juventus defender Sandro Salvadore, the captain of the Italian side. That Italy's twenty-three and twenty-two-year old experimental Milanese striking combination Giovanni 'Gianni' Rivera of A.C. Milan) and Alessandro 'Sandro'" Mazzola (of Inter Milan) should gel so well on their first outing together, and each slot their first international goals, was an unexpected bonus.

Italy bottled up Eusébio for seventy minutes at Ayresome Park on Friday 9th July. A crowd of 28,657 saw a fascinating tactical battle gradually evolve and then unwind, with the Portuguese playing nearly all the football with the Italians threatening every now and again to pick the lock and steal the game. It was Eusébio who broke the deadlock in the seventy-second minute and captain Mário Coluna who ecstatically swept in a second goal six minutes later. To their credit the Italians fought to the last minute, with Gianni Rivero passing the ball into the net over the body of the diving José Pereira to restore an air of respectability to the score line.

Needing to beat Colombia to stay in contention the Irish dropped Derek Dougan and reinstated Johnny Crossan at his home ground. The famous 'Roker Roar' amplified by the voices of 37,106 honorary Ulstermen drove Northern Ireland forward. Suffice to say that George Best scored the only goal he ever scored in a World Cup Finals tournament – an ugly, accidental affair with the ball cannoning off his left shin when he had his back to the goal after Johnny Crossan had miscued a shot from point blank range – to put the Irish ahead.

An own goal late in the game looked to have scuppered all hope – Alex Elder inadvertently heading a cross past his own keeper – before the hero of Roker Park, Johnny Crossan found the net with a diving header with eight minutes still on the clock. The match had been a scrappy, entertaining affair which meant that nothing short of a victory against Portugal on the following Tuesday might; hoping against hope that Italy drew with or lost to Colombia the following evening could prolong Northern Ireland's interest in the tournament.

The Irish went down fighting in front of 35,881 strangely muted spectators at Roker Park. Afterwards,

George Best claimed 'it was like playing at home at Windsor Park in Belfast but louder'.

The Irish gambled, playing both Derek Dougan and Crossan up front, and lost, gallantly, but comprehensively. The match was as good as over by half-time.

Eusébio scored a hattrick in the first twenty-nine minutes, Mário Coluna made it four-nil on the hour and although George Best drifted in and out of the game with brief dazzling interventions, a Johnny Crossan shot which went into the Portuguese net after deflecting off Fernando Cruz's shoulder was no real consolation.

On the evening of 13th July Italy surgically stifled and then picked Colombia's pocket, Sandro Mazzola scoring twice, goals separated by a Gianni Rivera penalty.

GROUP 4	P.	W.	D.	L.	For	Ag.	Pts.
Portugal	3	3	0	0	9	3	6
Italy	3	2	0	1	6	2	4
Northern Ireland	3	1	0	2	3	7	2
Colombia	3	0	0	3	2	8	0

This meant that the Uruguayans were destined to travel up to Sunderland to face Eusébio and company at Roker Park in Quarter-Final no. 4; with the victors going forward to play either Brazil or Spain in the Semi-Final at Villa Park on the 18th July.

Meanwhile, for the Italians a clash with Argentina at Hillsborough awaited; with the winner of that match going on to face the victor at Wembley, either England or Scotland at the Commonwealth Stadium in the Semi-Final.

The preliminaries were over.

The real battle for the Jules Rimet Trophy was about to begin!

15 | Quarter-Finals Day

Saturday 16th July 1966

Throughout the tournament England were the guests of the Guards Depot at Pirbright in Surrey, at that time the home of the much-expanded Coldstream Guards following the reorganisation of the Brigade of Guards the previous autumn. The title 'brigade' was a hangover from before the October War; all four Guards 'Regiments' now mustered five, six or seven battalions 'of foot' and plans were in hand to create a combined armoured brigade capable of fielding over a hundred main battle tanks based around Salisbury.

The Pirbright camp had been much expanded to serve as the Regiment's training, recruiting and rest centre, while the Scots Guards had removed to Edinburgh, the Welsh Guards to Hereford and the Grenadiers to Catterick in the North Riding of Yorkshire.

That summer 1st and 3rd Battalion Coldstream Guards were in France, 2nd Battalion was on ceremonial and security duties – in Oxford, Woodstock and providing a 'guard company' for the National Army Logistics base at Abingdon - 4th Battalion was on exercise in the Brecon Beacons in Wales, elements of the 5th Battalion and the Regiment's Communications and Intelligence Company was in Northern Ireland, the 6th, recently returned from the Mediterranean was in the process of assimilating new recruits and replacements at Pirbright, and 7th Battalion had recently embarked for a six-month tour of duty in Portugal, one of a number of unannounced, although not actually very secret redeployments of men, aircraft and ships designed to reassure the Portuguese in the wake of a spate of recent Spanish-provoked border incidents and renewed 'threatening noises' coming out of Madrid. Such incidents, 'provocations' mounted by Falangist – Franco's fascistic militia – had flared periodically since the Anglo-Spanish war of December 1963. By the summer of 1966 Portugal had become a 'warm weather training ground' for the British Army, Lisbon and Porto Airports had become the biggest RAF outposts in Europe outside the United Kingdom and transiting Royal Navy warships rode in the waters of the Tagus and Douro Estuaries most days.

Although nobody seriously believed that the Spanish wanted a new war, or even to escalate troubles along its shared border with the Salazar regime; the days when anybody in Oxford took *anything* for granted had ended long before the dreadful developments in the United States at the start of the year.

What with one thing and another living hand in jowl with the Coldstream Guards somewhat 'kept our feet on the ground' Jimmy Armfield was to recall. In fact, the England team was in daily contact with base personnel, many of whom were wounded, injured or sick men recently returned to light duties proudly wearing their scars.

More than one footballer reflected how bizarre it was that '*they* looked at *us* as if *we* were the heroes!'

Alf Ramsey, who always regarded his own experiences in the Army in the Second World War as among the happiest of his life, was never more relaxed than when he was at Pirbright that summer. His men gave each other funny looks and in private, took the 'mickey' out of their chief for the way he 'sirred' and often seemed on the verge of saluting Guards officers; but there was something deep in Ramsey's psyche that remembered, no matter the situation on the field, that football was just a game and that the men at Pirbright were the ones who were actually fighting the 'real' war. Nobody was asking an England footballer to go out and die for their country; at Pirbright the footballers were surrounded by men who might be ordered to do just that at any time.

The period leading up to the tournament and during it was a cloistered time for the players of all the nations involved; there was visceral hostility to the Argentines, the Spaniards and – let us not mix our words – no little racism in the attitudes to, and behaviour towards the men from several other countries.

That summer there was an upwelling of prejudice against Italians in the community, even visiting Scottish supporters were abused and there were isolated mini-riots involving and frequently provoked by roving gangs of youthful 'home' supporters.

It serves to remind us that all was not peace and light

in the United Kingdom in that period.

A lot of people south of the border – sadly, it was a generally felt misconception, a travesty of the truth – believed that the Scots had 'got off lightly' and been, in some non-specific way, slow to come to 'England's aid' in the months after the recent war. Many resented how quickly life in Scotland had returned to 'normal' while people in England were starving and freezing to death in bomb-wrecked cities. It was a myth; Scotland more than 'did its bit' when the going was toughest!

In that first, terrible post-war winter of 1962-63 it was Scottish volunteers flooding south in their thousands who propped up the surviving rail network in the north of England, kept roads and ports open, and abandoned their own warm hearths and families to come south to keep what survived of the National Health Service running. Moreover, throughout 1963 and afterwards Scots flocked to the colours and welcomed as many as a million refugees from the stricken lands to the south.

Today we look back on that glorious summer forgetting that on the opposite side of the North Atlantic a continent was in ferment, that the United Kingdom was fighting a war in France and that across the whole Northern Hemisphere from the plains of Central Europe to the cold waters lapping on the rocky shores of Taiwan conflict threatened, flared, or went on unabated and that the British Archipelago, for once in its long and troubled history, was not so much beyond the worst of the storm but briefly within its great, swirling hurricane eye.

Saturday 16th July dawned brightly across much of the country; only in the North East did a raft of high cloud slowly sweep in from the North Sea bringing spits of rain and the promise, unfulfilled of thundery squalls. Elsewhere the sun blazed down upon a nation seemingly in the thrall of 'World Cup fever'.

Thousands had camped out overnight at Wembley Park ahead of the England versus Scotland clash. By now David Willison and Miriam Prior's planning ensured that the vast camp ran like clockwork, the masses were well fed and watered, guarded and stewarded by soldiers and policemen in shirtsleeves, unarmed, and the casualties inevitable among a transient horde, many of whom had smuggled in bottles of beer and other 'hooch' were well cared for by the staff of the Wembley Combined Services Mobile Field Hospital in the shadow of the Commonwealth Stadium.

As many as thirty babies were born in the temporary hospital at Wembley Park during the tournament. It was the nearest – properly equipped and staffed – medical facility for miles around and women came to it during and in the weeks after the World Cup was over to give birth. The gardens of the modern Wembley Park Cottage Hospital are sited where the original tented temporary hospital was located in 1966.

Other people came to Wembley Park for a variety of reasons.

A small minority came to rob and to prey upon fans distracted by the football, those who were caught were given short shrift by the authorities. For a miscreant justice was summary and not long delayed; a spell in a bread and water regime at the nearby holding centre – little more than a barbed wire cage close to Wembley Central Station - run by the Redcaps, the Royal Military Police, before assignment to a work gang or banishment to a normal civilian prison at which hard labour, was de rigor what awaited the majority.

The War Emergency Acts made no attempt to pay, other than lip service, to the pre-war 'niceties' of the legal system in place in England and Wales. Justice could be, and was often, brutal. In July 1966 looters or persons defying local curfews or trespassing on military or caught within the boundaries of nominated 'strategic stockpiles and depots' could, and still were, shot on sight. Ongoing fears of terrorist attacks – either by the Irish Republican Army, or by one or other of the cells of Red Dawn fanatics, such as the suicide squad which had assassinated Secretary of State for Defence William Whitelaw, MP, and his wife during the spring 1965 election campaign, still believed to still be operating in the British Isles, had led to a trigger-happy culture among troops and policemen guarding vital installations, offices and persons, and much as one is loath to say it, in some circumstances life in the summer of 1966 could still be very 'cheap' in England.

The whole nation had been traumatised by the recent war; understandably sensibilities were dulled, and to an extent not really understood nowadays, few of the survivors, hardened by deprivation and grief cared a jot for the harsh treatment routinely meted out to 'freeloaders', 'criminals' and 'traitors'.

However, the vast majority of people came to Wembley Park to enjoy the party, to share in the atmosphere of the camp. They travelled for days, sometimes for hundreds of miles by foot, bus, train and foot again to reach north west London in countless personal odysseys that later became the subject of myth, legend, and innumerable articles and books, and even movies. Although nobody knew it at the time a new post-war folklore was in the making, moulded from the ashes of the great, stricken city around the twin citadels of the Commonwealth Stadium in the west and the Boleyn Ground in the east.

In describing what was, pre-October 1962 the Greater London Area, it is hard now to get one's head around the idea that an area of some five hundred square miles had been laid waste on the night of the war and in the days thereafter, by the subsequent firestorms. But already in the fourth year after the cataclysm, a remarkable metamorphosis was in progress spurred by the very permanence of the two mighty castle keeps amidst the ruins, two bases from which all else for miles around was eventually to spring, rejuvenated with the same spontaneity with which nature had begun to 'green' the thermonuclear wasteland of the old metropolis.

People began to reminisce about the 'Ration Book' Olympiad of 1948 when London had resuscitated the Olympic movement in the wake of the Second World War. Practically speaking, John Joe Mears and his Organising Committee, Miriam Prior, David Willison and Ted Dexter had taken those games – held in a country bankrupted by the war and still living under forced austerity – as their model for many of the preparations for the World Cup tournament. Back in 1948 the Olympic Games had given the country something to celebrate, something to be proud about and the footballers of 1966 had achieved exactly the same result.

For the first time since the Cuban Missiles disaster the newspapers were filled with interviews with visiting players, and even with a few of the hardiest of the small number of visiting supporters. Suddenly, there were unfamiliar accents on the radio, and the BBC included pieces about this or that match or team on every news broadcast. In cinemas Pathé and the Ministry of Information rushed the latest snippets of action, of footballers performing party tricks in training, or snatches of the Italians or the Brazilians caught in moments when they were normal tourists.

There were publicity stunts aplenty much to the embarrassment of the Home teams; in one the captains of the four British sides toured Wembley Park 'meeting and greeting' soldiers, policemen, medical staff and other workers before being mobbed by crowds of back-slapping well-wishers and autograph hunters. The England Captain, Jimmy Armfield took it all in good spirit, John Greig his Scottish counterpart was stiff and uneasy in comparison.

Ironically, the English press had canvassed for a 'tougher man' than Armfield to lead out the national team. But that was to mistake the Blackpool defender's personability, approachability and impeccable manners with a lack of toughness; Armfield was the perfect professional and self-evidently, decent to the core and the man in the street instantly connected with him. Never the most spectacular of players he was steady, without obvious weaknesses without ever being the star of any team in which he played but that was immaterial, for he was the heart and soul of that England team and without him to steady the ship in times of trial the side was holed beneath the waterline.

Inevitably, all the attention on Quarter-Finals day was on the England-Scotland match at the Commonwealth Stadium but each of the four matches was a potentially mouth-watering, fascinating prospect for any connoisseur of soccer.

The second Quarter-Final at Hillsborough between the evenly matched Argentines and Italians promised to be a dour, cagey affair hopefully enlivened by flashes of Latin magic. Not to be discounted was the possibility it might descend into a pitched battle of attrition determined by how many men were still standing at its conclusion. In that event Argentine brutality was almost certainly likely to be countered with Italian angry bravura; nonetheless, it was plain that both sides had men who could turn any game with a split second of inspiration.

In Birmingham, Brazil were the runaway favourites to dismiss the Spanish challenge. However, the Villa Park match was no foregone conclusion. The Spanish were a well-marshalled team whose men had not had their careers broken by the cataclysm, many of whom had been playing together all their adult lives. If the Brazilians were not at their best, or worse, off their game or complacent, the Spanish were quite capable of inflicting a famous upset on the Champions. Such was the beauty of the knock out phase of any competition.

Finally, there was the intriguing meeting of the effervescent Portuguese – cheered on by the Roker Park faithful they had entertained so royally in their group matches – against the impregnable, unambitious Uruguayans whom, like Argentina, had yet to concede a single goal in England. Could Eusébio and Simões and company break down the South American wall?

The day of the Quarter-Finals, Saturday 16th July 1966, is now remembered elsewhere – universally, more or less – as being the day two terrible battles raged thousands of miles away but in England, for once, all the blood and thunder was on the green summer sward of four famous old football grounds, and the only roaring was not of engines of war but from tens of thousands of throats.

In the 'big picture' the World Cup Finals of 1966 were a footnote to history, a tiny mote of relative sanity in the madness of the world.

Today great sporting events can seem to dominate the news; not so in 1966 and we forget this at our peril.

16 | The Panthers of Roker Park

PORTUGAL versus URUGUAY
(Roker Park, Sunderland)
Attendance: 36,004

The opening minutes of the match confounded the expectations of the 'experts'. Far from digging in for a long defensive campaign the Uruguayans sprang from the starting blocks like greyhounds and initially, knocked the Portuguese completely out of their stride.

The South American's very own Eusébio, José Eusébio Urruzmendi Aycaguer – more prosaically known as plain José Aycaguer, very nearly scored, actually he should have, when he latched onto an uncharacteristically casual back pass from Mário Coluna that not so much sold goalkeeper José Pereira short as shot him in the foot. The look of anguished relief on the Portuguese Captain's face when just seven minutes into the game José Aycaguer's angled shot clipped the base of the near post and went harmlessly behind was a thing to behold!

A few minutes later Pereira fumbled a long-range thunderbolt from Peñarol striker Pedro Rocha - another extravagantly talented man who would have walked into three-quarters of the sides in the 1966 tournament - that looked as if it was heading goalward until Sporting Lisbon's left back Hilário - Hilário Rosário da Conceição - lashed it away as it was literally crossing the goal line.

The Uruguayans immediately surrounded the referee, Englishman James Finney.

A Lancashireman, forty-one-year old Finney had refereed the last pre-October War FA Cup final at the Empire Stadium in 1962, after which Tottenham Hotspur skipper Jimmy Blanchflower had presented him with the match ball. Well-respected in England with experience of refereeing and running the line at several internationals, suddenly being mobbed by a whole team of violently gesticulating, threatening Latin Americans must have been a wholly new experience to the man who had recently resumed his pre-war non-football career as the travelling representative of a Manchester brewery.

'I would have sent somebody off but they were all as bad as each other!' He confided to work mates a month or so later.

The linesman overseeing the Portuguese half had been unsighted, and in any event had been fifteen yards behind the play at the critical moment, so he was no help.

'The ball might have been over the line but,' Finney admitted, 'but a referee can only give a goal if he thinks the whole of the ball is over the line, he can't guess!'

So, Finney did not guess.

Some four minutes later he re-started the game with a dropped ball in the centre circle.

The Uruguayans had, if one may use a modern vernacular 'lost it big time' by then. Pedro Rocha, still clearly incensed by the non-goal made no attempt to win the ball from the 'drop' but took a kick at Mário Coluna who fortunately, saw it coming and stepped away in time.

Finney booked Rocha and with what seemed, at the time, tragi-comic inevitability, two minutes later sent him off for bowling José Pereira to the ground in the six-yard box. The Portuguese keeper had picked up the ball and was bouncing it as he looked up field for a target to throw or kick to. In that era a goalkeeper could not carry the ball, instead he had to bounce the ball as he moved. While it probably was not, de jure to challenge the keeper (i.e., shoulder to shoulder), it was generally accepted that you just did not do 'that sort of thing'. One certainly did not physically assault a goalkeeper moving about his penalty area bouncing the ball!

It was also true that in that era, practically anything went vis-à-vis challenging the goalkeeper for the ball *when it was in play*; however, once the goalie had the ball in his hands that was that although now and then burlier centre forwards had been known to attempt to 'shoulder charge' a man into his own goal.

Rocha sealed his fate by standing over the prostrate Pereira threatening to kick him if he did not spring straight back up to his feet. He did not actually kick his man when he was down, instead he settled for nudging the man on the ground with the right toe of his boot...once or twice.

'OFF! OFF! OFF!'

Again, Finney was surrounded.

The Uruguayans fell apart after that.

Allegations of English bias against South American teams were being muttered by half-time; and shouted by Uruguayan squad members in the stand by the finish.

The miracle was that James Finney booked seven Uruguayans without sending off two or three more. The real pity was that the controversy partly overshadowed the masterclass - of what years later everybody would call 'total football' – Portugal laid on for those lucky enough to be inside Roker Park that Saturday afternoon.

Everybody expected every Brazilian to control the ball with a single deft touch, carry it with utter security, pass it precisely, to run like an Olympic athlete for ninety minutes without drawing breath, to head and to strike the ball with irresistible power, now beneath darkling northern skies the Portuguese were outdoing the Champions.

Eusébio ran onto a Simões cross to volley in the first goal in the thirty-second minute; and for the rest of the half this rallied the Uruguayans as shots rained in on Ladislao Mazurkiewicz's beleaguered goal. The twenty-one-year old Peñarol keeper had got a hand to Eusébio's strike, pushed it onto the inside of the post to no avail, otherwise his heroics alone kept the score down to a single goal at the break.

The floodgates opened as the first squall of a short-lived summer storm rolled in from the east driving the hardy souls on nearby Roker Beach running for shelter. It was the first summer since the war that people had come down to the bleak beaches around the mouth of the River Wear, begun again to rest from the humdrum battle for survival, and begun again to hope to enjoy rather than to endure their lives. The North East had not been bombed but there was little comfort in that in a country half-broken, grief-struck and afflicted with illnesses and maladies once imagined relegated to the darkest corners of ancient history. Roker Park had become a temple of remembrance to the days before the cataclysm, a place where once or twice a fortnight people might flock to forget their woes, and to re-live again their dreams.

So, when the Portuguese ran riot, playing as if their sole object was to entertain and to thrill as if this was a friendly exhibition match, and eventually crashed, headed and passed four more goals into the hapless Uruguayans' net heedless of the slashing tackles and flying studs of their outmatched opponents, the roar of the terraces anointed Eusébio and his immortal Panthers.

The big, unnervingly mobile and swift-footed centre forward José Torres, scored a hattrick, and Simões the fifth goal falling upon a Eusébio cross-shot which had evaded Mazurkiewicz's left hand. Torres - José Augusto Costa Sénica Torres – Eusébio's hunting partner at Benfica was to terrorise club and international defences for the rest of the decade but never again score a hattrick in a Portugal shirt.

Rightly the Portuguese triumphantly performed a lap of honour after the final whistle. Sunderland had come to love them as their own and who was to say that Roker Park had not just witnessed the future World Champions in action?

This was hardly implausible; not least because unlike most of the other teams Portugal had come this far without losing a man to a serious injury.

Potential injuries and illness were headaches for all the teams.

At the insistence of Mexico and the South Americans no team was permitted to replace a sick of an injured man during the tournament; since this was a thing easily done by the England and the other 'home' countries but, given the exigencies and the uncertainties of global travel at that time, impractical for most of the visiting countries with the theoretical exception of the Portuguese, the Swedish, the Swiss and the Ghanaians who had been flown to England by the RAF. The Italian and Spanish teams had been obliged to travel to England by sea, and the Latin Americans had flown across the Atlantic from the United States. For the Uruguayans, Argentines and Chileans this had involved as many as four connecting flights to get to New York's Idlewild Airport before finally boarding a Pan Am flight to either Prestwick in Scotland or Brize Norton in Oxfordshire, and journeys of as many as three to four days including much idle waiting around for connecting flights at airports which – in that era – had few diversions or amenities available to even VIP travellers.

Thus, when a side lost a man to a serious injury – or,

given the compressed nature of the tournament, any kind of injury which did not heal itself in a day or two – it had to fall back on its existing resources and make the best of a bad deal.

However, many who watched the Portuguese limp off the field after their walking-jogging, unhurried lap of honour wondered how many of those heroes would be fit in the morning, or in time to play in the Semi-Final at Villa Park in *only* two days-time.

17 | Pelé!!!

BRAZIL versus SPAIN
(Villa Park, Birmingham)
Attendance: 41,207

In footballing memory, the names of the Brazilians in that side still reel off the tongue like a list of heroes from some lost, mythic age. Not quite Odysseus, Hector, Menelaus and Achilles perhaps; but as near as damn it!

Yes, a gap was opening between the old guard of 1958 and 1962 and the youngsters coming through but that Brazilian team was a seductive, seamless blend of experience and precocious youth and seemed unstoppable. The old, the new and the future of Brazilian football was represented in that side which met Spain at Villa Park.

Gylmar, that most calm and catlike of goalkeepers anchored the side. Then in his thirty-sixth year Gylmar dos Santos Neves, had played his domestic football for Corinthians and then Santos, and kept goal in both the 1958 and 1962 winning sides. His powers were undimmed in 1966.

Nowadays, we might regard Palmeiras legend thirty-seven-year old Djalma Pereira Dias dos Santos as being 'past his prime' at the top level. But Djalma Santos had been for a generation the best right back in world football and this was his fourth World Cup.

On the left flank was a man some thirteen years' his junior destined to be very nearly Djalma's equal, Botafogo's twenty-four-year old Rildo da Costa Menezes, much better known as just 'Rildo'.

It was as if the master and his most accomplished apprentice were in the same defence, one elegantly marshalled by Hilderaldo Luiz Bellini, Brazil's thirty-six-year old veteran captain. And next to Bellini in the heart of the defence was Fluminense's Altair - Altair Gomes de Figueiredo – another man from the victorious 1962 campaign in Chile.

Insofar as Brazil believed in the need for dedicated defenders, that was that. There was no such thing as a Brazilian who did not run like a Cheetah and tackle like a terrier, although if the team had a chink in its armour it was that here and there legs were not quite as young as they had been in 1962, and there were – at least 'notional' - gaps in a defence whose job was, most of the time, simply to watch the action unfolding at the other end of the pitch.

Botafogo's midfield general twenty-five-year old Gérson de Oliveira Nunes – Gerson – combined in the engine room of the eleven with another veteran, thirty-three-year old José Ely de Miranda, more commonly known as simply 'Zito'. Zito was Pelé's Santos club captain and with Gerson and Garrincha there was no more creative or inventive trio in the game.

No man in world football was thirty-two-year old Manuel Francisco dos Santos's - Garrincha – equal with the ball at his feet. When he carried the ball, it was as if it was literally, tied to his boots, time and again he would ghost past the most resolute of defenders as if they were so much Scotch mist. He had played over six hundred senior games for his club, Botafogo, scoring nearly two hundred and fifty goals and debuted for his country eleven years ago. But for Pelé he would have been the most famous footballer in the World. Such was the man who wove his spell on the Brazilian right wing.

Playing on the left, biding his time to claim his favoured position when Garrincha eventually hung up his boots was Garrincha's twenty-one-year old Botafogo team mate Jairzinho - Jair Ventura Filho – all muscular endeavour and blazing pace with jack hammer strikes in both feet.

Playing in the space between *Little Bird* and Jairzinho was the fleet-footed, goal-poaching Cruzeiro star nineteen-year old Eduardo Gonçalves de Andrade – Tostão – and without a doubt the greatest footballer of all time, Edson Arantes do Nascimento, or to his adoring fans and admirers wherever he went, the incomparable Pelé.

The sensation of the 1958 finals and one of the men of the 1962 tournament the free-scoring, dazzling leader of the Santos and Brazil attack was still, in July 1966, only in his twenty-sixth year. He had first played for his club aged fifteen and for his country before his seventeenth birthday, in both club and international football he had scored at a rate of a goal a game from the outset, a strike rate hardly inconvenienced by the fact that he had been the most marked man in the game all his career.

The Spanish must have felt like the whole world was gainst them as they walked out that day!

The really frightening thing about the Brazilians of that era was that they could play with a complacent, laid back mindset for much of a game and win it in ten mesmeric minutes at the flick of a switch. They were the only side in the tournament which had not two but five or six gears; and were capable of suddenly switching up from idling along in first or second gear to sixth gear in literally, the blink of an eye. Slow, slow, slow, a sudden blistering acceleration, a wicked cross ball or through pass and the ball was in the net and everybody was looking at each other asking: 'what just happened?' It was as if it was all too easy, a little boring and that sometimes the 'magnificos' needed a sharp jab in the ribs to wake up and, as we might say today, 'smell the coffee'.

José Sánchez, the twenty-one-year old Real Madrid prodigy already nicknamed 'Pirri' made the mistake of doing exactly this – giving the Brazilians a 'wake up' call - in the fortieth minute of an otherwise strangely pedestrian first-half, latching onto a deflection from Spain's first corner kick of the match. Until then the Brazilians had been strolling around the field as if the match was a training session, completely in command.

Stung into action both Pelé and Jairzinho might have scored in the closing five minutes of the opening period. After the break the World Champions imperiously buried the ball in the Spanish net three times in seventeen minutes before resuming their gentle training session, seemingly saving their legs for the Semi-Final.

Tostão began the scoring, lashing in a lay back from Pelé from fifteen yards out. Next, Pelé rose imperiously above the Spanish defence to head the ball down and over the diving keeper's hands. Three minutes later Gerson rifled the ball into the top right-hand corner of the net from over twenty-five yards out. It was clinical, brutal, and utterly merciless all at once.

The Spanish huffed and puffed, tried to get back into the match and near the end José Sánchez – his team's man of the match – might have snatched a second goal, Gylmar palming his sharp strike onto a post in the eighty-eighth minute.

There was no shame in being out-classed by Brazil.

It was one of those performances where opposition analysts learn little other than how to hold their heads in their hands in despair. Spain had not played badly; but Brazil had hardly played at all for over three-quarters of the match and yet won at a canter.

How did one counter sheer, unadulterated genius?

Such was the problem now confronting Brazil's next opponents, Portugal, in the Semi-Final at this same ground in just two days' time.

18 | Into the Trenches

ITALY versus ARGENTINA
(Hillsborough, Sheffield)
Attendance: 33,738

'Absolutely nothing happened in the first-half', one reporter wrote in the next day's edition of *The Sunday Express*. This was not entirely true; both teams had been introduced to the Lord Mayor of Sheffield Lionel Farris and the Chairmen of the Sheffield Wednesday and Sheffield United clubs and their wives before the match.

And Argentina's Ermindo Ángel Onega had kicked off.

It was only *after* that which nothing of note happened.

Both sides had come to defend and hopefully, score a goal on the break. 'Cagey', 'tactical', 'cerebral' are all terms carelessly employed to describe the kind of cat and mouse, riskless, unambitious approach of the sides in contests of this type. The only words which do this kind of football justice are probably 'boring', or 'pointless'. Neither team had come to Sheffield to entertain the crowd populating the Hillsborough terraces in the blazing afternoon sunshine; if it had been a boxing match the referee would have stepped in to demand that the pugilists 'get active' or abandoned the fight as a 'no contest'.

It was painful to watch; the sort of game many supporters stop watching with more than half an eye and fill the empty minutes chatting to their friends and neighbours, or more productively shouting encouragement to or abuse at the participants in the farce.

"Nothing much was going on but there was still a lot of *niggle*," match referee Ken Dagnell recalled. Like the other English referee in the 1966 tournament – every team had nominated one man but England as hosts had provided a 'panel' of two referees and five other officials to 'run the line' as required – James Finney, Dagnell was a practical, common sense Lancashireman.

Away from football he had worked as a housing officer for the Bolton Office of the Ministry of Supply ever since the October War with special responsibility for finding 'billets, lodgings and shelter for refugees'.

Even the trials and tribulations of refereeing Argentina versus Italy was to be light relief in contrast to the endless travail of human misery and suffering he had witnessed in recent years.

Before the tournament it had been mooted that either he or Finney would referee the Final; assuming England were not in it. But all that was a long way from Ken Dagnell's mind that afternoon in Sheffield.

'If it had been a League or Cup match in England, I might have said something to the players. You know, a light-hearted *buck up your ideas* sort of dig but you didn't do that sort of thing with foreign players," Dagnell lamented. 'You couldn't, much was the pity!'

He had booked a player from each side in the first half.

'Just for a bit of *afters*,' he remarked ruefully. 'Both sides seemed to like to *have a piece of a bloke* if he had the nerve to dribble past him. Don't get me wrong, English pros were no angels but they were just more honest about their skulduggery, I suppose. They'd clatter straight into, and through, a man. But that day it was all from behind, and I hated it when players spat at each other."

The first flashpoint of the second half came when Boca Juniors' defender Silvio Marzolini chopped down Gianni Rivera – according to one's national perspective just inside or just outside the Argentina penalty box.

Ken Dagnell never hesitated.

'The tackle went in a split second after Rivera's right foot landed *inside* the box!'

He pointed straight to the penalty spot and was quickly mobbed by incensed Argentines.

Silvio Marzolini later claimed he slipped; that was incidental, because whatever the cause he shoved Dagnell in the back straight into the arms of the enraged Antonio Rattin. The Argentine Captain, Antonio Rattin was so surprised he forgot he was supposed to be protesting and caught the referee, stopping him going down to his knees and momentarily, was actually – in a vaguely chivalric fashion – solicitous for Dagnell's dignity and health.

One of the men running the line that day was Jack Taylor, already one of the most respected officials in the

English game. He had seen what had happened from the other side of the field and energetically 'flagged' at a somewhat shaken Ken Dagnell.

'The number four ran up behind you and pushed you, Ken,' he reported.

'What do you think?' The referee asked, still gathering his breath and his wits and a little shaken up after being pursued most of the way to the touchline by the entire Argentina team.

'He's got to go!'

Thirty-six-year old Ken Taylor was a Wolverhampton butcher by profession and had applied to the FA to officiate at matches in the re-formed Northern League in mid-1963, quickly being promoted linesman in the Football league in 1964. During the 1965-66 season he had refereed over thirty matches including the Manchester derby at Old Trafford that spring. His youthful, fit, imposing presence – he was tall and well made – inspired confidence in players and fans alike, and he was already well known for not being afraid to make difficult decisions.

Taylor followed Dagnell back onto the pitch and stood behind his back as he sent Silvio Marzolini to the dressing room. Even Antonio Rattin had seen this coming and although there were further protests after about five minutes Gianni Rivera slid his penalty shot into the bottom right hand corner of the Argentine net.

Eleven-man Italy promptly set about locking out ten-man Argentina for the rest of the match.

There was a certain inevitability that the equaliser, when it came, would also be from the penalty spot; on this occasion two Italians – Inter Milan's Giacinto Facchetti and Bologna's Romano Fogli – both handled in eventually keeping a Rattin header from a towering corner kick out of the net.

Several Italians were voluble in their protests but this time the guilty parties did not have their heart in their complaints and Ermindo Onega crashed the ball past Enrico Albertosi's flailing left arm with nerveless violence. The Peñarol striker would have performed an ecstatic lap of honour around Hillsborough had not he been ecstatically tackled to the ground by his team mates near the Italian's left-hand corner flag!

Practically everybody was so distracted by the celebrations that hardly anybody saw the origins of the scuffle in 'Ricky' Albertosi's goal mouth in which the goalkeeper manhandled Oscar Mais to the ground and half-a-dozen players fell into a fist-milling brawl.

However, the eagle-eyed Jack Taylor had seen it all.

'Who threw the first punch?' Ken Dagnell inquired wearily.

Five minutes before the end of the scheduled ninety minutes Giacinto Facchetti was trudging off the field. His ruggedly handsome features were creased with anger and he was spitting with every step.

Oscar Más meanwhile, was still prostrate on the ground in the Italian goal mouth – having 'headed' a goalpost as he was charged to the floor - and the Battle of Hillsborough had barely begun! The nineteen-year old striker was still being helped to his feet when Ken Dagnell blew up for full-time.

As the managers and trainers came onto the pitch to gather their players in huddles ahead of the forthcoming two fifteen-minute halves of extra time, Oscar Más, clearly still dazed sank back down onto his knees as supporting hands released him. Out came the magic sponge, then a bucket of water was poured over his head; he had no idea where he was and only the vaguest idea who he was, nevertheless, he was pushed back onto the field.

It was indeed, another age...

It was a hot afternoon, the sky cloudless and both sides in that age when substitutions – whether for injury or tactical reasons – were not permitted, were spent. A man would run for the ball, rest for several seconds, hands on hips or knees before attempting to run again.

The first half of extra time passed in dreary, slow-motion without either side threatening the other's goal. In 1966 there was no 'golden goal' or 'penalty shootout' if the teams ended level; in that event the referee would toss a coin and one of the captains would call 'heads' or 'tails' and that would be that.

It made for grim watching.

Both sides trotted, walked mostly, intent on keeping the opposition at long-range. Ironically, Oscar Más was far too concussed to understand any of the subtleties of the situation. He swayed and stumbled, ignored by many of the Italians on the fringes of the eighteen-yard line, oblivious to much of what was going on around him.

Afterwards, Oscar Más did not remember scoring the winning goal.

The ball broke to him twenty-five yards out, he ran onto it – purely from muscle memory we must assume – and somehow the ball got between the onrushing Albertosi and the near post moments before both the goalkeeper and Torino's Roberto Rosato crashed into Más like two runaway express trains.

It was not until the young Peñarol striker regained full consciousness in the Royal Hallamshire Hospital that night that he discovered that he was a national hero.

However, for this youthful hero the World Cup of 1966 was already over. His fractured jaw was wired up and his left forearm was broken in two places beneath the bulky cast which he would forever more regard as a badge of honour from his painful time in England.

As the match ended in a flurry of wild tackles and Italian and Argentine players pushed and shoved each other as they left the field, exchanging insults, kicks and punches in the tunnel to the dressing rooms; the Football Association's Organising Committee and the Government began, with no little dread, to ask themselves: what on earth was going to happen when Argentina walked out at Wembley on the coming Tuesday evening?

19 | Auld Enemies

ENGLAND versus SCOTLAND
(Commonwealth Stadium, Wembley)
Attendance: 98,303

England and Scotland matches – at whatever level – were not for the faint-hearted, if not quite nature red in claw and tooth, then they were traditionally as much tests of a man's moral as his footballing mettle. The two teams had played the first ever international football match, a goalless draw at Hampden Crescent in November 1872 - not to be confused with the original Hampden 'Park' where Scotland defeated the English 7-2 in March 1878 - and little love had been lost between the sides since.

In the ninety-two-year history of the fixture the two sides had won famous victories and suffered ignominious defeats; and given the vastly greater resources available to the English, overall the scales had been relatively evenly matched down the years.

However, in the ten years before the October War interrupted the annual hostilities the Scots had had but a single victory over the *auld enemy*, at Hampden Park in April 1962. Previously England had won seven of the preceding fixtures and three had been drawn, scoring thirty-three to Scotland's thirteen goals and in 1961, had beaten the visitors 9-3 at the Empire Stadium! The Scots' record at Wembley since 1951 had been bleak, four defeats and a draw.

Notwithstanding, Scotsmen pointed to the 5-2 drubbing of Alf Ramsey's experimental England eleven in Glasgow earlier in the year but that had been in the bullring of Hampden Park, and while it might be only three hundred and forty miles as the crow flew from Wembley it might as well have been a thousand or a million miles away for all the relevance of *that* match. Or that at least, was the English riposte.

The fact of the matter was that there was no reliable form guide, no relevant yardstick against which to compare the two teams; although neutrals – few that they were – tended to read more into Scotland's performance against the Brazilians than they did into any of England's group matches.

The only thing most people agreed upon was that on paper England looked the more solid defensively, and Scotland by far the stronger, and more adventurous attacking force and that on the wide-open spaces of the huge Commonwealth Stadium pitch that might just be the decisive factor.

Remarkably, there was very little of the gung-ho tub-thumping 'we shall overcome' mentality that England teams tend to attract these days. Moreover, although there was a natural excitement that England had got through to the quarter-finals, it was mitigated by a degree by a sense that whatever happened next was a bonus, sport was not in those days 'life or death'; it was...just *sport*. Not that one would have suggested such a thing to the six to seven thousand mainly Glaswegian brave hearts spurred on by the skirl of the highland bagpipes who trekked all the way down to the ruins of London from north of the border in a raggle-taggle convoy of buses and on the three special trains laid on at twenty-four hours' notice as soon as the quarter-final line-up was confirmed.

To many the first stirring of the 'Tartan Army' – more a regiment in its first manifestation – would be one of the brightest memories of that summer!

Of the two managers Alf Ramsey was the man with the problems. He had lost one striker, West Bromwich Albion's Derek Kevan to a shoulder injury against the Spaniards, and another, John Connelly had 'torn' his left hamstring in training two days before the Scotland match. Worse, several of his men were nursing knocks, unable to train between the Ghana match and the quarter-final. The walking wounded reported for duty on the morning before the big day but that still meant both his first-choice strikers were hors de combat; so, on the day of possibly the biggest match in England's long footballing history when the eyes of the world – or rather, of that part of the world which was not presently tearing itself to pieces – was on Ramsey's two fit strikers, Geoff Hurst and Brian Clough, men with six caps between them, the last of Clough's having come seven years ago.

What made it worse for Ramsey was that, as everybody had predicted, he and the outspoken, always opinionated and fiendishly sharp-witted Sunderland goal-scorer had had 'words' when Clough had not been given a 'run out' against the Ghanaians.

Basically, Clough was not Alf Ramsey's kind of team man and Ramsey had taken the younger man to task over this the day after the Ghana match. Clough was not a 'squad man'; he hated sitting around with no real prospect of getting a match. Clough had told Ramsey that Kevan and Connelly were the same kind of forwards and that it was a mistake to try to play them together. Geoff Hurst was in a similar mould, although better in the air than either of the older professionals and willing to take any kind of battering to win and hold the ball so that supporting players could catch up with play around him.

Now with both his first-choice strikers injured Ramsey had had no option but to bring in his troublesome 'spare' goal-scorer to play alongside Geoff Hurst in the most important match of his brief international managerial career.

At Ipswich Ramsey had acquired the reputation of being a manager who washed his hands of troublemakers; you did things his way or you moved on, or more often, down.

That was one of the reasons so many eyebrows had been raised by Brian Clough's inclusion in the squad. One can only wonder what it cost the England Manager to take a deep breath – probably a score or so – bite the bullet and put Clough's name on the team sheet for the Quarter-Final.

ENGLAND	NO.	SCOTLAND
G. Banks (Leicester City)	1	**C. Forsyth** (Kilmarnock)
D. Howe (West Bromwich A.)	2	**T. Gemmell** (Celtic)
J. Armfield (C) (Blackpool)	3	**A. Hamilton** (Dundee)
P. Swan (Sheffield Wednesday)	4	**P. Crerand** (Manchester United)
J. Charlton (Leeds United)	5	**W. McNeill (C)** (Celtic)
N. Stiles (Manchester United)	6	**J. Greig** (Rangers)
A. Ball	7	**J. Johnstone**

(Blackpool)		(Celtic)
B. Clough	8	**J. Baxter**
(Sunderland)		(Rangers)
R. Charlton	9	**A. Gilzean**
(Manchester United)		(Dundee)
G. Hurst	10	**D. Law**
(Southampton)		(Manchester United)
K. Flowers	11	**C. Cooke**
(Wolverhampton W.)		(Aberdeen)

Let it not be forgotten that Jock Stein, Ramsey's opposite number had his own problems.

'We could beat anybody on our day,' he would remind listeners sternly. 'Anybody. But we had to pick our day!'

Stein was a much harder and oddly, yet more forgiving taskmaster than Ramsey. He was also a lot less bothered about what people thought about him or his methods.

Stein knew that if Scotland managed to play the game in England's half for even a third of the game his front men had the beating of the auld enemy. In Denis Law and Alan Gilzean, he had strikers who scored goals for fun, and with Jim Baxter calmly managing the game from midfield and Jimmy Johnstone and Charlie Cooke on the wings Scotland were always – unfortunately, nearly always only on paper – full of goals.

Before the match the teams lined up below the Royal Box to be presented to Her Majesty the Queen, making her second visit to Wembley in a fortnight and by Sir Stanley Rous, the President of FIFA. The Band of the Royal Engineers played God Save the Queen and marched off, their boots sinking into turf sodden that morning after an overnight summer storm which had taken the edge off the sultry heat afflicting southern England in the latter part of the previous week.

On account of the presence of the monarch two RAF helicopters – Westland Wessex gunships circled the stadium throughout the match – and armed men in the kilts of the Black Watch fingered their FN L1A1 SLRs right up until the moment their charge was whisked away at the conclusion of affairs.

In post-cataclysm England nobody even noticed.

In the first minutes Billy McNeill and John Greig

made crunching tackles on Geoff Hurst and Brian Clough 'just to let them know we were here,' John Greig often smiled in the re-telling of the story of that famous day. 'Hurst jumped straight up; when you managed to knock him down, that was. There was less brawn about Brian Clough but he was silky quick over the first two or three yards although he never tried to hold the ball up the way Geoff would.'

There was a world of difference between honest hard tackles and being cut off below the knee by a scything assault from behind, or a man deliberately going 'over the ball' to rake and hurt one. There were no complaints that day.

No quarter was asked or given. The pace slowed after a frenetic opening ten minutes. The crowd paused for breath, the players re-appraised their foes and the Scots began to feed the ball to their wingers, Charlie Cook on the left and Jimmy Johnstone on the right. Of the two Cooke was elegant, sometimes languid and everything happened faster than observers realised at the time; Johnstone on the other hand was busy, busy, like an itch no defence could scratch, put him down and he would bounce up and the ball might have been glued to his right foot.

It was a little against the run of play that England scored.

Bobby Charlton collected the ball mid-way into the Scottish half, took one, and another step and swung his right foot and Campbell Forsyth was left clawing at thin air as the net behind him bulged.

The Commonwealth Stadium erupted in celebration.

England's lead lasted less than five minutes. Charlie Cooke cut in from his wing and sent a daisy-cutting cross across the face of the England goal which Alan Gilzean's left big toe got to the split second before Gordon Banks fingertips.

England responded the way they always responded to adversity at Wembley; they pressed forward in slow, remorseless waves pressing the visitors back and bombarded the Scots with crosses; and after every attack re-formed, closed down space and hunted down the ball again. Starved of service Gilzean and Law back-peddled in search of the ball, lived off scraps, hoping for a chance to counter-attack. One such opportunity fell to Alan Gilzean, had it fallen to the swifter Law, it might not have been snuffed out seconds before the whistle called a temporary halt to proceedings.

It was England that started the better in the second half and Ron Flowers's fifty-seventh minute goal, a cross shot through a crowd of players that wrong-footed Campbell Forsyth was no more than England's dominance deserved.

Both Geoff Hurst, heading wide when it would almost have been easier to score, and Brian Clough, unable to get the ball out from under his feet on the six-yard line ought to have scored and put the contest beyond doubt before the seventieth minute.

Emboldened by their good fortune the Scots rallied against opponents who had suddenly run out of energy and ideas.

Oddly, Denis Law had never been such a prolific goal-scorer as his striking partner. Gilzean, the only man playing at the top level of football in the British Isles who could match Brian Clough's near goal to a game scoring ratio, had only played in Scotland to date but that did not detract from his predatory efficiency in front of goal.

It was just that there was always something indefinable about Denis Law that marked him out as being *different*. He was not that big, five feet nine or ten, built lithely, his legs almost spindly for a professional footballer. Like Clough he was 'an awkward so and so sometimes,' although Law was more of the 'cheeky chappie' joker than the argumentative Yorkshireman and there could never be any question which of the two men had had more fun playing the game.

'If he had worked harder, off and on the pitch, he would have been an all-time great,' said one of his managers, only a tad tongue-in-cheek. Putting his nose to the grindstone was not Denis Law's way and had it been, he might not have been half the finisher that, on his day, he was.

Law had two half-chances to score, one in each half.

The first got away from him; the second, three minutes from the end of normal time he back-heeled into the net from seven yards out while everybody around him stood watching, rooted to the spot like statues.

Both sides had walking wounded by then.

England's Ron Flowers thought he had cramp, actually he had torn his left calf muscle so badly that he would be out of football for the first weeks of the 1966-67 season which began in August. For the Scots Charlie Cooke was attempting to run off a dead leg, but like Flowers he was to be a virtual passenger throughout the next thirty minutes.

Other men were already battling cramp; a common thing on Wembley's verdant, springy sward.

The two captains tossed a coin to decided which side should kick off extra time.

'I hope we're not going to be doing this again in half-an-hour to decide who goes through to the semis, Billy,' Jimmy Armfield grimaced as he tossed the coin.

Billy McNeill, appointed Captain that day, 'probably Jock Stein's way of geeing up John Greig', one team mate chuckled years later, called heads and lost, the second time he had called wrong that day. The Celtic stalwart hoped it was not an omen.

The game had barely restarted when Jimmy Johnstone slung in a low missile from the goal line and Alan Gilzean's prematurely balding head sent the ball looping over Gordon Banks into the England net.

It was around five in the afternoon and mercifully, cloud cover was forming over the bombed city taking the edge off the pressure-cooker heat of the late afternoon. Several players had recklessly gulped down water at the end of the normal ninety minutes; dehydrated they became light-headed, and a couple of men were seen to be sick on the hallowed turf.

Suddenly Brian Clough went down like a house of cards in the area; the referee an unsmiling Chilean waved play on. The Scots, fearing the worst as John Greig had not so much tackled as fallen into and over the England striker hesitated, wondering why they were not appealing for clemency in the aftermath of the award of a penalty kick. In that moment Alan Ball, the one man on the field who had never stopped running picked up his head and saw Bobby Charlton making a run towards the box.

Ball rolled his pass between the still prone Brian Clough and John Greig, too late Billy McNeill saw the danger as Charlton swooped and the ball flew past

Campbell Forsyth to bring the scores level.

It was not only the players who were suffering from the heat and the anxiety; the great crowd was by turns ecstatic, despairing, moribund, wilting and disbelieving as the two well-matched sides played out their epic encounter in a spirit oddly devoid of the niggling, antagonistic edge that had characterised so many past meetings down the years.

One wonders what agonies the radio audience of millions must have suffered that overlong afternoon in July?

The stress of it all played havoc with the voice of one of the BBC's radio commentators that day at Wembley; by the end thirty-four-year old Brian Moore's voice was so hoarse, his vocal cords so misused that he had to hand over commentary to his colleague Maurice Edelston.

'The occasion got to us all,' he later confessed. 'Most of the Scottish defenders were out on their feet when Geoff Hurst ran onto Nobby Stiles's hack down field. I think Nobby and Alan Ball had covered every blade of grass that afternoon, and I remember Nobby going down with cramp as if he had been shot the moment, he thumped that ball in Geoff's direction.'

Hurst of course, just went on running.

In retrospect, that was the match that meant he was always a first pick in any Ramsey team thereafter. As any manager will testify, once you find a man who will run through brick walls for you, you stick with him through thick and thin.

Geoff Hurst hurdled Archie Gemmell's despairing lunge and as Campbell Forsyth came out to narrow the angle, he rolled a slide-rule pass into the path of Brian Clough and in the one hundredth and seventeenth minute England finally got their noses in front.

Billy McNeill drove his men forward on the field and Jock Stein stalked the touchline like a bear with a sore tooth; to no avail, players sank to their knees at the final whistle in exhaustion.

In that moment of victory and defeat there was no jubilation on the England side, shirts were swapped and even Alf Ramsey – that most detached of figures throughout the tournament – stood aside when his men stuck their heads inside the Scottish dressing room and the first bottles of beer were uncapped.

Briefly, Englishmen and Scots had been sporting enemies; now with the battle fought they could all be 'in this thing together again' and after what they had all been through since October 1962 that, was the only thing that really mattered.

20 | The Semi-Finals

The Fédération Internationale de Football Association, the Football Association and by the next morning Ted Dexter's Ministry of Sport and Recreation, and in no time at all the Foreign and Commonwealth Office and the representatives of over a dozen diplomatic legations in Oxford were to become embroiled in one of the biggest rows in football history.

Yes, I know...it might have been the biggest row in football history...but...trying to name the 'biggest row' in football is a bit like trying to make up one's mind what was the biggest 'row' in the millennium-long history of the Byzantine Empire!

Except harder!

But anyway...the allegation was that European officials were biased against Latin American nations, with whom defeated *European* quarter-finalists Spain (relatively quietly) and Italy (loudly and very plaintively) both sided with, and with contrary vehemence also took issue. But what were the actual points of contention which landed like a clutch of hand grenades – minus their firing pins – at the door of the World Cup 1966 Organising Committee and in no time at all, on the Prime Minister's desk.

'What the Devil is going on, Joe?' Ted Dexter is alleged to have demanded after his office had put through a call to the Chairman of the Football Association after he was button-holed by his Permanent Secretary at the Ministry for Sport, Robin Butler just before he and his wife were due to leave his residence overlooking The Parks to attend the morning service at Christ Church Cathedral.

That day the Dexters had been invited to lunch at Hertford College as guests of the Prime Minister and her husband, a huge feather in the former England Cricket Captain's political hat and an implicit nod to his part in the huge success, to date, of the World Cup, not least in the way it had temporarily distracted the bulk of the British people from the new terrors being visited upon the world at that time.

'It's the South Americans, Ted," John Joe Mears had groaned in exasperation. He and Dexter had got on famously after a wobbly start; and out of the company of the other footballing moguls, whom Mears knew had a knack of rubbing the Minister up the wrong way, he and the younger man had been on first name terms ever since the Prime Minister had given the World Cup 1966 'project' her seal of approval a year ago. "They don't trust European referees and they've all put in complaints about their accommodation and training facilities. Several of the teams have protested about security arrangements; they claim they don't feel safe,' he had snorted contemptuously at this point, 'as if any of us is *safe* these days! Anyway, all the teams due to go home this week want new *security guarantees* and apologies for the way they've been treated while they've been over here...'

Ted Dexter admitted to being flummoxed at this juncture.

He was aware that there had been an 'incident' involving the Argentina team bus in Sheffield after the match with Italy but he was still awaiting a report on that, otherwise things seemed to have gone off fairly well.

The contract under which all teams had agreed to accept invitations to compete in England that summer had been signed, with appropriate minor amendments to facilitate entirely reasonable Brazilian, Argentine and Mexican demands with regard to their 'safety' in the spring. Everybody had known what to expect and that the tournament was being mounted in 'trying and testing circumstances'.

So far as Dexter knew 'appropriate measures' had been taken to deal with the concerns of the visiting teams.

That morning, John Joe Mears, was as much in the dark about the seriousness of the 'Sheffield incident' as the Minister for Sport and Recreation.

'This is nothing to do with football, Ted," Mears observed sourly. 'Well, I'm not quite sure what the Italians and the Spanish are up to, but the Argentines are the real problem...'

'I don't understand,' Dexter confessed. Throughout, he had fastidiously kept out of internal football squabbles praying that nobody was going to come to him and ask him to arbitrate in judgement a-la Paris or King Solomon. He often got those ancient, mythic fellows confused but then it was always a tricky thing in olden days knowing which appellant to chop in half or have stoned to death. That the Chairman of the FA had felt moved to call him boded nothing but ill.

'The Latins have had a bee in their bonnet about getting a rough deal from European officials,' John Joe Mears reiterated, 'right from the start. The Argentina-Italy match has set them all off! I'm not quite sure if the Italians are on the Argentina side; it's all a bit mixed up at the moment. They're both screaming about Ken Dagnell and Taylor, he was the linesman, our boys at the match yesterday, either favouring the other lot, or not being hard enough on foul play. Both sides kicked each other to pieces, anyway. Dagnell probably decided to let them get on with it; otherwise it would have ended up as five or six-aside at the end, and then there were the penalties. The Italians put in a letter to the organising Committee demanding Argentina be expelled for quote 'kicking them out of the World Cup' first thing this morning. Although, they withdrew that demand without a by-your-leave half-an-hour ago!'

Dexter's mind had finally started working like a real politician in the last few months. Initially, he had been a bull in a china shop, not really knowing what was expected of him in the Government. With Robin Butler's help and the advice of senior colleagues he had gradually grown into his role; now he was thinking several steps ahead, calculating the risks and re-drawing his 'red lines'.

The Prime Minister had only flown back into Brize Norton at three o'clock that morning after her secret three-day mission to the United States to confer with President Nixon and Canadian Premier Lester Pearson. Dexter himself had only learned about the 'Big Three Conference' convened onboard the USS Enterprise at Placentia Bay, Newfoundland, the previous evening. Apparently, his leader had crossed the North Atlantic in company with the Foreign and Commonwealth Secretary, the Chief of the Defence Staff, General Sir Michael Carver, the Chief of the Air Staff, Air Chief Marshal Sir Christopher Hartley and a large supporting cast including the Directors of Operational Planning of all three of the armed services, leaving First Minister of State and Deputy Prime Minister, Lord Carington, holding the reins.

The story had been put out that the Prime Minister

was 'visiting the troops in France' and that seemed to have been swallowed by the media. Given the reverses suffered recently by allied forces in central France and in the fighting below the Loire-Line on the Biscay coast nobody, even in the Manchester news rooms of the national dailies expected the Ministry of Defence to advertise Mrs Thatcher's itinerary in advance in a potential battle zone. The Cabinet Office had warned all departments to expect a major policy announcement at ten o'clock tomorrow morning.

However, Dexter could hardly tell the troubled Chairman of the Football Association that!

He took a deep breath.

"What are we up against, Joe?"

"The Argentines are threatening to pull out. If that happens the Brazilian junta will probably order their chaps to boycott tomorrow night's Semi-Final at Villa Park."

"What do we do it that happens?"

The older man had not expected such a direct question.

"I don't know, Ted."

Interviewed for this book nearly half-a-century later a glint of mischief still twinkled in Ted Dexter's eyes recounting his conversation with Joe Mears.

'England, Argentina, Brazil and Portugal were the only teams left in the competition. For two of them to pull out this late in the day would have been an embarrassment; but the Argentine junta had left it too late to completely wreck the tournament. I think Joe Mears, and I know Rous [Sir Stanley Rous] and Harold Thompson were worried about the fallout from the row within FIFA but frankly, I took the view that was their problem. Portugal was our staunchest ally in Western Europe; we had several thousand Navy, RAF and Army people based in Portugal and as many Portuguese over here, at Sandhurst, studying in our universities and working in a whole raft of Anglo-Portuguese enterprises. Whatever happened, Portugal would have no part of any walk out or boycott. If Argentina and Brazil packed their bags and departed then England would meet Portugal in the World Cup Final come what may.'

Mears had been less gung-ho.

'What if Argentina and Brazil win their Semi-Finals and boycott the Final next Saturday, Ted?'

'Then,' the Minister of Sport decreed, 'the losing Semi-Finalists will be invited to contest the Final.'

'I'm not sure we can do that...'

'I'm sure the word 'default' appears on most of the pages of the contract that all the teams signed before the tournament.'

'Well, yes, put that way...'

'Joe,' Dexter had explained gently to the Chairman of the Football Association, 'I have no intention of explaining to the Prime Minister why *we* are even talking about giving in to pressure from the Argentine.'

Nonetheless, the first thing Dexter did was ask Robin Butler to find out what had happened in Sheffield the previous evening; his newly acquired political nous warning him that something must have prompted the sudden heightening of tensions and he doubted if it, whatever it was, had a great deal to do with events on the field of play.

'That,' he would joke, 'was a useful insight I learned captaining England in Australia. Nothing is ever quite what, on the face of it, it seems to be!'

In those days being sent off in a match, or the accumulation of bookings did not automatically result in a ban, or necessarily a sanction of any kind. Before the October War in international matches FIFA theoretically had the right to convene disciplinary panels to sit in judgement of miscreants but there was no such provision in England in 1966. To have instituted such arrangements would have involved endless haggling and player disciplinary matters had not been high on anybody's list of priorities. Therefore, such matters were entirely at the discretion of national football associations.

Nevertheless, immediately after the Italy game the Argentine dressing room was like a casualty clearing station and by the next morning at least seven men – including four who had been in the starting line up less than a fortnight before – were on the injury list.

Had they still been in the tournament the Italian situation would have been even more dire since they had only brought nineteen players to England; having selected their quarter-final team from an 'available squad' of only fourteen players which included both the squad's goalkeepers.

At this remove one can sympathise, if not support in every respect, the heightened emotions of the time. For the Argentina team the trip to England only a year after the war in the South Atlantic, and what seemed to its players – all of whom were ignorant of, and to a man had had absolutely no part whatsoever in any of the atrocities blazed across British newspapers and constantly referenced on the radio and TV – was a crusade to defend national honour. From the moment they stepped onto English soil they had felt themselves to be maligned, threatened, among enemies and the British Government's failure to do anything about the abuse and frankly, racist harassment and taunting that Argentina were subjected to at every venue, was in hindsight, despicable; a thing often forgotten but that shamed us all that summer.

Ted Dexter was mortified to learn what had befallen the Argentine team after the Hillsborough semi-final.

No footballer deserves to be pilloried for the excesses of its ruling regime or military. The miracle is that the Argentine footballers 'held it together' for so long, not that in the end they snapped. Twice the Argentine team bus – despite its heavily armed escorts – was stoned by mobs whilst leaving a match; most disgracefully in the streets of Hillsborough an hour after the end of the Italy match. The policemen and troops responsible for the safety of the Argentine players had been granted the authority to use whatever force – including lethal force – was necessary to ensure the 'absolute security' of ALL the teams participating in the tournament. In both cases the Argentine team bus was attacked the local commander was unwilling to authorise his men to fire on the mob.

That Saturday evening one of the men injured by flying glass from his bus's broken windows was Argentine Captain Antonio Rattin, who later required five stitches for his head wound.

When the Prime Minister was briefed by her Minister for Sport on Sunday morning about what had happened, she too was horrified.

'Actually, that was the only time I was with her when she was well, incandescent with anger,' Dexter remembers.

That afternoon she penned a personal letter of apology to the manager of the Argentine team, Juan Carlos Lorenzo, which was handed to him on his 'safe' arrival at the Commonwealth Stadium on the afternoon of Tuesday's Semi-Final.

In her letter she assured Senior Lorenzo that the Royal Marine protection detail she had assigned to protect his team *'will remain with you for the rest of your time in England. I give you my personal word of honour that the shocking scenes in Sheffield will not be allowed to happen again...'*

The measure of her affront may be deduced from the fact that she promptly instructed Major Sir Steuart Pringle, the head of her own legendary AWPs – Angry Widow's Praetorians – to temporarily hand over command to his deputy and to 'take as many Royal Marines as you need to do the job to look after our honoured guests from the Argentine'.

Within hours the most hated men in England were under the protection of over a hundred of the elite fighting men whose Royal Marines brothers in arms had been humiliated and murdered on the Falklands Archipelago a little over two years ago by other Argentines on the Falkland Islands...

It was indeed a funny old world sometimes...

Steuart Pringle did not hesitate to order *his* men to fire over the heads of the threatening mob which had assembled at one point along the road through the ruins on the Watford-Wembley road to 'greet' the Argentines.

Initially, this had the required effect.

However, later when a larger, more threatening mob attempted to waylay the Royal Marine-Argentine convoy – and the first missiles were thrown - Royal Marines shot three men dead, and injured at least eleven others, and liberally dispensed tear gas to disperse the troublemakers; thereafter, no more bricks or bottles were to be thrown at a visiting football team in England for over twenty years.

Back in Sheffield the officer who had failed to protect his charges was subsequently court martialled for neglect of duty and cashiered.

Popular folklore maintains that Juan Carlos Lorenzo tore up the Prime Minister's letter in disgust. Antonio

Rattin contradicted this at the time of the 1970 World Cup Finals in Mexico; Lorenzo had read the letter to the team before the Semi-Final against England, and for many years it was prominently displayed in his apartment in Buenos Aires in a frame made from wood taken from a goal post at the ground of the River Plate club he managed in the latter 1960s.

In retrospect the miracle was that Argentina chose to battle on to the bitter end rather than to pull out of the tournament. Undeniably, had the competition dragged on for five or six weeks in the manner of modern 'finals' there might have been time for fears and tensions to fester, for Governments to score points, and for those who wanted to wreck the World Cup Finals of 1966 to plot and scheme its ruination.

As it was the ludicrously compressed time scale – with everything done and dusted inside three weeks – probably saved the FA, FIFA and the international game from a generation-long schism.

21 | The Beautiful Game

Monday 18th July 1966
BRAZIL versus PORTUGAL
(Villa Park, Birmingham)
Attendance: 44,554

Brazil and Portugal were the two teams which had thus far avoided serious injuries, arriving in Birmingham only two days after their respective quarter-final triumphs bruised and a little heavy-legged but otherwise with full-strength squads. By then the claustrophobic life living in a cocoon separated from, in the main, the dangers of everyday life in England in those days was beginning to prey on the minds of men far from home, homesick and mentally if not physically wearied by the brutal schedule of match after match.

In those days cities and towns tended to be safe havens, enclaves in a landscape where travel between centres of population was sometimes like – to employ a movie analogy - taking a stagecoach through hostile country. Parts of the country were more lawless than others; in mid-1966 nobody batted an eyelid if a soldier or a policeman shot a suspected looter on sight, especially if there was a local curfew in effect. Irish Republican terrorism, although low-level and sporadic, was in everybody's minds. There were still many places where strangers simply did not dare to go; and while the majority of people welcomed the visiting footballers, there were many who resented their presence and the scarce food and resources being 'wasted' on their upkeep.

The country had been in chaos in the winter of 1962/63 and the Government had only been able to extend its writ across the whole land incrementally in the following three years. No policeman in the British Isles would dream of going on duty without a firearm; respect for authority was horribly fragile and could never be taken for granted, and British society as a whole had in some respects, been brutalised, and partially-inured to suffering by its struggle for survival. How could it be otherwise when two great cities, London and Liverpool were devastated boneyards, and other towns had been obliterated and so many places touched, scorched, changed forever by the fire?

The return to 'normal' standards, normal life, normal feelings, normal loyalties was going to be a generational project. So, there was never any prospect of visiting footballers freely, or unescorted meeting 'real' people, or seeing what sights remained to be seen in England. They lived in their secure camps, travelled through often dangerous country under guard, played in mostly hostile stadia and returned again to their armed camps without ever meeting a 'normal' human being outside of their own tight-knit tribe.

It was undoubtedly worse for Argentina but for the other eleven teams from abroad it was only better by degree; for all through no fault of their own shared the same manner of incarceration. Alone among the 'foreigners' the Portuguese were welcomed, treated almost as an honorary 'Home Country' by the crowds who flocked to the stadia of the North and the Midlands. Now that the exploits of Eusébio and his dazzling compatriots had begun to appear in every cinema and in 'recorded highlights' endlessly replayed on the nation's million or so black and white televisions kids in the street now wanted to be Eusébio as much as they idolised Pelé.

Although the BBC began trial broadcasts as early as 1967 colour TV sets were not added to the 'Approved Importation of Manufactured Goods List' until 1974, coincidentally at the same time Ferranti-Marconi opened a factory producing sets capable of fully utilising the roll-out of UHF 625-line transmission.

In those days when there were few private cars, and surviving younger children were being 'spoiled rotten' by families who now invested their whole being in the future of their offspring, adults watched over, and coached the putative would be George Bests, Bobby Charltons and all the other new heroes of that halcyon July hoping, almost for the first time with a dash of optimism, of a better future for their sons and daughters.

Brazil had been a vast Portuguese colony, then an independent Portuguese South American Empire before breaking from Lisbon. Now it was a military plutocracy of a modern kind, unlike the older, wearier brand of António de Oliveira Salazar, the last and least mendacious of the European dictators. The two nations spoke a common language and the Salazar regime in the old country had reached out to the Brazilian junta before even the United States – which everybody assumed had been behind the Army coup led by Field Marshal Humberto de Alencar Castelo Branco - which abruptly ended the Second Brazilian Republic in the spring of 1963.

Brazil had travelled to England via Portugal in June to play two friendly matches against a combined Benfica and Sporting Lisbon eleven and a full international against their hosts. Afterwards, although the Thatcher Government had offered to fly the Brazilian team to England with the Portuguese, the Branco regime in Brasilia had turned this down, so Pelé and company had had to take a slow boat from Lisbon to Southampton.

The exhibition match against the 'Team Lisbon' had ended 7-4 in the visitors' favour. The meeting between the two full-strength national sides at Benfica's Estádio da Luz – *Stadium of Light* – in front of a crowd of over a hundred and twenty thousand people, had ended in a 2-2 draw.

Given that Portugal had lost all five of the previous meetings with Brazil – albeit all bar one of those defeats by only a single goal – the formbook, such as it was, was therefore heavily in the Brazilian's favour. However, reports from Lisbon dwelt upon witnesses claiming that the Portuguese had 'over run' their guests for long periods of that encounter and had they not relaxed in the last quarter of the game when they led by two goals to nil, they might have won a famous victory.

On the other hand; how many points do you get for winning a 'friendly'?

The two sides had never met in the latter stages of a World Cup. Today's match was new territory for both sides and given their progress thus far in the tournament – they were the two best teams by a mile – it almost seemed unfair to pit them against each other short of in the Final itself.

Her Majesty the Queen and Prince Philip had travelled to Birmingham to review the teams before the kick off, and to watch the match from the much 'gentrified' Directors' Box in the company of the

Portuguese Ambassador, whose Brazilian counterpart had refused a similar invitation. Nobody had troubled the Queen with the details of any of the ongoing 'difficulties surrounding the South American teams'.

Now that the country was back on a firm democratic footing after the previous year's general election the monarch had retreated to Blenheim Palace at Woodstock and done her level best to be again the constitutional Head of State she had been schooled, since childhood, to be ever after.

In the immediate post-war crisis and the crises which followed in 1963 and 1964 the Queen had asserted ancient Royal prerogatives in what she construed to be the national interest. That was then and this was now and she had no intention of dipping her toe in the murky, shark-infested waters of high politics again!

Given the inflated expectations and the raw goal-scoring power in opposition that warm evening in Birmingham, it ought not to have been a surprise that both teams started tentatively. Simões struggled to get behind the Brazilian defence, in the centre José Torres was initially out-muscled and two Brazilians instantly closed down Eusébio every time the ball came near. Meanwhile, Garrincha began to unfurl his dribbling skills, Tostão and Pelé ran circles around bemused full backs to no real effect. The football was 'pretty', tactical, for the purist absorbing but lacking in real spirit. It was still goal less at half-time and the crowd, torn between supporting the Portuguese allies or applauding the World Champions, had never really found its full, throaty voice.

It was as if both sides had used the first forty-five minutes to test out their opponents. Each emerged from the Villa Park dressing rooms with new, high energy plans that were oddly alike. Suddenly, everything was happening at pace, tackles were thudding in and in the melee, Eusébio charged through, rode goalkeeper Gylmar's challenge, stumbled and walked the ball into the Brazilian net.

José Torres added a second goal in the fifty-third minute, a neat header from a Mario Coluna cross in one of those moments when every defender in the penalty box thinks that somebody else is going to challenge the header of the ball right up to the second that...nobody jumps with the danger man.

Two goals in less than five minutes which threatened to prise Brazil's hands from the Jules Rimet Trophy so worthily held for the last eight years.

The Brazilians seemed a beaten team.

Thirty-seven-year old Djalma Santos had been 'skinned' on the outside by Mario Coluna; thirty-six-year old Hilderaldo Luiz Bellini, Brazil's captain had watched Eusébio skip past him like a panther in the night and been able to do...nothing. On the wing thirty-two-year old Garrincha suddenly looked as if he was trying to negotiate a six-feet tall brick wall, the *Little Bird's* tricks were being nullified by the athleticism, nimbleness and swarming numbers of defenders; while on the opposite wing Jairzinho was hardly getting a touch of the ball.

But Champions never surrender.

Enter Pelé the magnificent!

Taking down a ball on his chest he was instantly into his stride. Three, four, five ground-devouring paces, and at a sprint he lashed the ball past a helpless José Pereira from at least twenty-five yards out.

In that split second the Portuguese bubble burst and the reigning World Champions caught a second wind. Brazil had looked down and out, out-paced, out-muscled and out-thought; yet a moment of genius had flicked a switch, turned the match upside down and now it was as if the apprentices were about to be put in their place. Time and again the ball traced intricate, swift, then slow, slow, fast patterns across the Villa Park turf.

José Pereira fended off two, three blistering shots, another skimmed the cross bar, Pelé headed a ball from point blank range into the goalkeeper's torso before, on the seventy-minute mark, gliding a perfectly weighted ball along the ground into Jairzinho's path for the twenty-one-year old winger to equalise.

By now the sky was darkening and the Villa Park floodlights painted the men on the pitch in brilliant white light; there was no hiding place now, a single mistake, or miss stood between glory and the dark pit of defeat.

The Portuguese had been hanging on, chasing leather in their own half and were the last to realise that the dynamic had changed again. The Brazilians had clawed themselves back into the match by dint of sheer willpower; given everything and now they were part-spent, part-astonished that they had got back on even terms.

Later, it was learned that Pelé had pulled a thigh muscle in scoring his goal and that Djalma Santos played the last thirty minutes of the match with a knee injury that was to effectively end his career. Spectators only noticed how slow each man was to the ball, how gingerly they picked themselves up from tackles, and how they slowly faded out of the game.

António Simões made the decisive break in the seventy-ninth minute, evading a despairing last gasp Bellini tackle on the ten-yard penalty circle directly in front of goal and blazing a skidding shot to Gylmar's left. All the goalkeeper could do was parry the ball at José Torres's feet and the rest, as they say, is history.

Sport is cruel.

Replete with what ifs?

What if Pelé had not been injured?

What if Djalma Santos had been a few years younger?

Might the veteran defender had cut inside in time to block Simões's strike?

Portugal had dethroned the kings of world football.

The kings are dead; long live the kings!

22 | War by Other Means

Tuesday 19th July 1966
ENGLAND versus ARGENTINA
(Commonwealth Stadium, Wembley)
Attendance: 97,887

The England side that walked out in its alternative strip – red shirt, white shorts, blue-black socks – at a little before 7:15 that balmy July evening looked and felt, fit, quietly confident and was, after its hard-fought win three days ago basking in the warm glow of the nation's adulation.

'We were aware what was going on elsewhere in the world,' Bobby Charlton remembers. 'We couldn't let ourselves get distracted. If we were worried about things going on in America and Canada, or France or the Far East it was more to do with how that was going to affect our own families and friends at home. Alf [Ramsey] tried to keep us insulated from all that outside stuff that we couldn't do anything about. The feeling within the camp was that all we could do was to go as far as we could in the tournament and cheer up as many people as possible.'

It was Bobby Charlton's and England Captain Jimmy Armfield's quiet, modest, self-deprecating commentary on England's unfolding campaign which made by far the most lasting impression on the generations who lived through those times. The brash reminiscences of Brian Clough and others, mostly several years after the event, offer a different narrative but at the time Armfield and Charlton were the first men pushed into the limelight, the quiet leaders of Alf Ramsey's first great England team.

The Argentine eleven emerged in their vertically striped sky blue and white shirts, white shorts and socks carrying the wounds of their pyrrhic triumph at Hillsborough. A couple of men sported black eyes, others moved stiffly, but Antonio Rattin strode out like a Roman gladiator, a look of steely determination written on his face below the heavy bandages that protected his recently glass-gashed forehead. Another man similarly patched up was goalkeeper Antonio Roma, who brought up the rear of the line of grim-faced Argentines presented to the Queen and Prince Philip. Rattin and his men were unsmilingly respectful, heads were bowed. Their dignity prior to the kick off was in stark contrast to the behaviour of many in the packed stadium who had hissed and booed; and flung no little hysterical vituperation at the South Americans.

England too, were expecting the footballing equivalent of trench warfare.

Ron Flowers had been ruled out of the rest of the tournament with the calf muscle tear which had reduced him to a passenger in the Scotland match. Alf Ramsey had replaced an experienced attacking midfielder with Norman Hunter, a man more normally to be found plying a stopper's dark arts in partnership with Jack Charlton on the left side of the Leeds United defence. Otherwise, England were unchanged from the Scotland match.

Not so Argentina whose starting line-up included only five of the men who had featured in their first match against the Scots a fortnight before. Manager Juan Carlos Lorenzo had had none of the normal problems or dilemmas in finalising his team sheet; that morning he had thirteen – more or less fit - players, three of whom were goalkeepers!

Name	Position	Club	Age
Antonio Roma	Goalkeeper	Boca Juniors	34
José Varacka	Midfielder	San Lorenzo	36
Nelson López	Defender	Athletico Banfield	25
Carmelo Simeone,	Defender	Boca Juniors	31
Silvio Marzolini	Full Back	Coca Juniors	25
Oscar Calics	Midfielder	San Lorenzo	26
Antonio Rattín	Midfielder	Boca Juniors	29
Alfredo Rojas	Forward	Boca Juniors	29
Juan Sarnari	Midfielder	River Plate	24
Ermindo Onega	Forward	River Plate	25
Aníbal Tarabini	Forward	Independiente	24

Before the game Alf Ramsey suspected Argentina would opt for a four-four-two formation with Rattin probably dropping into the back four; or that the South Americans might even play five men in midfield with only a single striker, most likely Alfredo 'El Tanque' Rojas up front. Problematically, looking at their team sheet England's opponents were going to be so unbalanced that until the match was under way it was impossible to predict what to expect other than to brace for the expected rough house.

'Whatever you do,' Ramsey said over and over again to his men, 'do not retaliate. Do not go down to their level!'

Notwithstanding that nobody was looking forward to a feast of flowing, attacking football, the Referee's Panel of the Organising Committee had – in its wisdom – appointed Mexican, Rudolfo Matthias to take charge of the match, supported by linesmen hailing from Chile and Sweden.

Alf Ramsey had asked Sir Stanley Rous to request that a 'stronger man' be appointed. Rous had refused to intervene, possibly on the grounds that he might have been rebuffed and as with 'all senior football administrators the main thing is not the game but the preservation of their personal dignity and privileges'.

Anybody familiar with the subsequent history of FIFA will readily accept the voracity this unattributed quote!

The 'Referee's Sub-Committee' comprised only a single representative from the FA, its other members being a Brazilian, a Mexican, an Italian and a Swiss. The FA's representative acted as 'Chair' and tried desperately to avoid a situation where his was in any way a 'casting vote'.

The whole thing was one of the 'quiet' compromises John Joe Mears had made – much to Sir Stanley Rous's and Harold Thompson's ire – to ensure that the tournament actually took place. Most of the other compromises worked well, all things considered but 'I always knew the Referee's Panel might cause us problems later', he freely admitted shortly before his death, of a suspected heart attack probably hastened by a brush with that winter's virulent influenza on 3rd January 1968.

Argentina took control of the football virtually from the kick off, passing crisply, rolling the ball nonchalantly across the lush Wembley sward and methodically exploring the possible chinks of light in the England defence.

'We just chased the ball for the first twenty minutes;

we were keyed up for a fight and it didn't happen,' Jimmy Armfield remarked ruefully. 'Bobby [Charlton] grabbed my arm and said something like *we've got to start playing* but every time we tried, we ended up kicking long and giving the ball away again. Eventually, I told Norman [Hunter] to play twenty yards further up the field and to start using that left foot of his for something other than standing on. That seemed to get the Argentine's thinking; although not before time because we'd almost leaked a couple of soft goals by then!'

El Tanque had thumped one shot against Gordon Banks's legs, and the Leicester keeper had plucked another header practically out of the top right-hand corner of his net in the eighteenth minute.

Initially, Hunter's inclination to step infield threatened to leave a yawning gap on the left flank for the visitors to exploit; however, Argentina's ambitions were circumspect, and when at last England began to string coherent attacking moves together the wall of blue and white shirts fell back, with all thoughts of offence abandoned.

'Nobody laid a finger on me until five minutes before half-time,' Brian Clough remembered. 'I could look after myself when the ball was somewhere in the vicinity the problem was you couldn't have eyes in the back of your head the rest of the time!'

Antonio Rattin's head wound had opened up again by then and his white bandage cum bandana was painted red, his cheek dripping with blood.

Perhaps, that was what maddened him sufficiently to take a kick at Clough as he walked past watching play on the other side of the field.

'I'd have retaliated if I hadn't been so worried, I'd broken my bloody leg!' Clough complained.

The youngest and the shortest man in the England side, twenty-one-year old Alan Ball, was the first man on the scene. It was almost but not quite comical to see him squaring up to the much taller, blood-spattered Argentine Captain in the moments before every player on the pitch converged on the scene of the crime.

It went without saying that neither the referee or his assistants had seen a thing. Senior Matthias spoke hardly any English but with every appearance of solicitude he listened to Rattin's gesticulating account of the cause of the unpleasantness, and booked both Clough, still on the ground receiving treatment, and Alan Ball for ungentlemanly conduct.

Then he turned around and blew his whistle for half-time.

It was Jack Charlton who stepped in front of an irate Alf Ramsey as the England Manager marched onto the pitch to intercept the referee.

'He's not worth it, Guv,' the big man said philosophically. 'Cloughie will be all right, we'll sort them out in the second-half.'

True to his word the big man 'sorted out' Alfredo Rojas three minutes after the interval. *El Tanque* went down as if he had been hit by a car and true to form, Senior Matthias did precisely nothing except award Argentina a free kick.

Thus encouraged, Norman Hunter repeated the medicine on the unfortunate Rojas a couple of minutes later leaving his man in a heap on the touchline right in front of the Argentine bench.

It was one of those afternoons when it was not always obvious who the real villains were...

Re-bandaged and cleaned up but still wearing the same blood-stained shirt Antonio Rattin was a shadow of the monster he had briefly become at the end of the first-half; it was as if that act had temporarily extinguished his rage. The rest of his team seemed to take its cue from him. The scything lunges went back into the cupboard, out came the well-practiced hair-pulling, shirt-tugging, spitting, nibbling at heels, tripping men as they went past routines. It was sad because on the evidence of the first quarter of the game even weakened, with many of their best players missing, Argentina were a match – in pure footballing terms – for England and most of the other sides in 1966.

England pressed forward. Senior Matthias awarded ten free kicks in a row to the home side in the Argentine half as the pressure mounted. It was only a matter of time before one of the constant stream of free kicks or corners fell to at an Englishman's feet or met his head in front of goal.

It was Brian Clough who made the breakthrough in

the seventy-third minute. A Bobby Charlton piledriver ricocheted around between the penalty spot and the six-yard line before the ball came Clough's way and he buried it in the net.

Geoff Hurst headed in a second six minutes later, latching onto an Alan Ball cross delivered from the touchline before José Varacka – the veteran's pride shredded after chasing Ball's shadow all afternoon – tackled the little man so late it was very nearly posthumous!

Senior Matthias booked the Argentine.

Then he sent him off; apparently, for being rude to him about being booked.

'I think he only said 'Gracias',' Alan Ball would chuckle in later years. 'You know, saying 'thank you' in Spanish. But that referee was a waste of space. He was on the panel again in Mexico four years later but I don't think he got any of the big games...'

Geoff Hurst ran through Antonio Rattin to poke in a third goal with a minute left on the clock.

Brian Clough stood over the Argentine Captain, strangely detached from the celebrations beginning all around him.

'I'd kick you, now,' he explained phlegmatically, 'but I don't plan to be remembered for being the bloke who kicked a man when he was down. But I can wait until you get up if you want!'

Rattin had jarred his left knee trying to bring down Geoff Hurst.

'It is only football," he muttered, wincing in pain.

Clough shook his head.

'I was going to kick the bugger,' he maintained, 'but the next second the rest of the England team jumped on top of me and we were off on a lap of honour!'

Nobody attempted to swap shirts.

The well of sportsmanship was empty.

In any event at the final whistle if any England player had approached an Argentine player he would probably have been confronted with by a Royal Marine – Steuart Pringle's men had rushed onto the field at the end to escort his charges safely to the dressing rooms - with orders to shoot to kill first and ask questions later.

Pringle himself and three of his 'best bruisers' made

absolutely certain that nobody got close to, let alone had the opportunity to abuse or harm Antonio Rattin as scores of spectators fought their way past the stewards and the first lines of policemen to get onto the pitch.

The BBC later edited out the shots of pitch invaders being clubbed to the turf with rifle butts and booted feet prior to being led and dragged away by grim-faced Royal Marines and kilted men of the Black Watch.

Malcontents had been warned: the match day program had warned that anybody so foolhardy as to 'trespass on the playing area may be shot!'

That, after all, was the true measure of the insanity of the age.

23 | Arrivals & Departures

ARGENTINA versus BRAZIL
(Commonwealth Stadium, Wembley)
Match cancelled.

'Yes, Mr Rattin asked me if it was true." Steuart Pringle confirmed thirty years later when all the Cabinet Papers about the Falklands had been released. He and his charges had got on well, forming a man-to-man rapport in the ten days that he and his men were responsible for the personal safety of the Argentine football team and its small management and coaching staff.

The 'IT' in question were the stories about what had happened during and after the invasion of the Falklands Archipelago in April 1964.

Rattin and his fellows had thought the *Las Malvinas* campaign had been a short, clean, virtually bloodless war and that the subsequent removal of the British soldiers and the civilian population had been a peaceful affair overseen by the Red Cross. That was what he had been told, anyway, and since he was a proud Argentine patriot that was what he had believed.

Steuart Pringle had diplomatically 'marked his card' for him.

'I told him that I knew several of the chaps who had been killed during, or immediately after the invasion or were suspected to have disappeared in the weeks afterwards. I told him that British civilians had been held as hostages and executed by Argentine forces after the sinking of the aircraft carrier *Indepencia* by British submarines. When I told him of the abuse that a number of Falkland Island women had suffered at the hands of their captors he was utterly mortified. Initially, he refused to believe it. When it all sank in, I think, actually, he was a little bit surprised that he and the rest of the team had not been arrested yet.'

Steuart Pringle paints a wholly different picture of the man, and of the other Argentines he met during that period than that presented by the same men on the field, or the vicious characterisation of them in the daily papers, and down the years in popular memory.

'They were fathers, brothers, sons, they loved their country and they, most of them, were convinced that Las Malvinas were a part of Argentina, rather like we regard the Orkneys or the Isle of Man. They were proud that their country had taken back territory that was its by right. The oddest thing was that for some reason I could never really fully understand, they thought the whole thing was over, done and dusted for all time. They honestly believed that *we* would just sit back and accept the fait accompli. I think learning about the war crimes perpetrated before and after the 'Malvinas Campaign' came as a nasty shock but I don't think even that shook their belief that the war for the Falklands had been fought, won and was over.'

Footballers as a breed are not usually – insofar as they think about it at all – great geopolitical thinkers.

'But there I was, having quietly given my boys orders to fraternise and to get to know the minds of the Argentine players and I don't think it ever occurred to Rattin, or Senior Lorenzo the Manager, that I was, as a good Marine, extremely eager to learn whatever I and my men might about our once, present and future enemies.'

Perfidious Albion is and always was alive and well!

Losing sides always feel more knocked about than winning ones; nonetheless, Argentina would have been hard-pressed to put out a team to take on the mighty Brazilians in the traditional Third-Place Match at Wembley on the evening before the World Cup Final. That was less than two days away when the disconsolate Argentines trooped down the tunnel to their dressing room.

There were riots in Buenos Aires that night; the old, deserted British Embassy building was ransacked and set on fire and numerous businesses with British-sounding names – there were a lot of those in Argentina because the country had been settled by many people of Welsh stock – were attacked. Initially, the regime made the mistake of letting the mob have its fun; the next day Argentine militia and policemen fired live rounds into crowds outside government offices and military bases in the city to restore order. Buenos Aires was still under nightly curfew a week later when Antonio Rattin and his men returned home with all the fanfare of thieves in the night.

It later transpired that the President of the Argentine had sent an order to the team instructing it to pull out of the tournament three hours before the scheduled kick-off of the Semi-Final. However, the message was only received by Juan Carlos Lorenzo on the team's return to its secure compound at the base of the Parachute Regiment in Aldershot in the early hours of the next morning.

The Brigade Major of the Parachute Regiment, whose mother was Spanish and was able to speak the language 'like a native since childhood' apologised fulsomely.

'Nobody on duty yesterday afternoon spoke Spanish,' he explained, 'so they had no idea the communication was important. It did not help that we received it via the Americans and they removed all security and priority headers before they transmitted it to us. Obviously, had we known it was important we would have couriered it to you without delay.'

Thus, the Argentine's participation in the tournament ended with a whimper, not a bang. There would be no last stand, no final valiant act of defiance, simply the humiliation of having to accept their hosts' offer of a flight to New York, from whence their government would 'presumably, arrange transport home'.

Brazil, on the other hand, remained in England another week. The whole squad was invited to a reception at Blenheim Palace, and on their penultimate day in England the Brazilians were driven through Oxford on an open-topped bus as if upon a champions' triumph!

At the time Argentina were disqualified and therefore stripped of fourth place; Brazil meanwhile were spared a pointless match and officially deemed to have come third.

In a postscript to this unique footballing denouement, two years later the record was amended awarding Argentina 4th placed, and therefore the 4th ranked team in the World ensuring they would be seeded along with England, Portugal and Brazil in the top tier of the draw for the group stage of the 1970 finals in Mexico.

24 | The Final

Saturday 23rd July 1966
ENGLAND *versus* **PORTUGAL**
(Commonwealth Stadium, Wembley)
Attendance: 98,479

How would England deal with the 'total football' of the Portuguese Panthers? Nobody seriously imagined that Alf Ramsey would contemplate changing his 4-3-3 system, or 'monkey-about' with the team sheet beyond perhaps, tinkering around the edges. Most pundits assumed that Norman Hunter's selection on the left side of midfield in what, for most of the Argentina game had been a four rather than a three-man midfield was a one-game expedient; but 'you never knew with Alf' hardened football writers murmured under their breath.

When England announced an unchanged eleven there was much scratching of heads. The team looked like it was set up to play 4-4-2 and a defensive version of the formation at that! It had made a kind of sense against the Argentine, a tactical re-configuration to stop the South Americans passing down the flanks and pulling a three-man midfield from side to side, stretching the cover in front of the back four. Yes, it would make the pitch more congested for the Portuguese runners but, and it was a big but, how on earth did Ramsey think he was going to prevent Hurst and Clough getting completely isolated up front?

Not that such arcane considerations overly concerned the tens of thousands of mainly home supporting spectators packing into the Commonwealth Stadium on that bright, sunny afternoon.

High in the South Stand the former Soviet para-trooper Anatoly Saratov and his English wife Greta soothed their nerves munching the sandwiches they had brought with them from their small, sparsely furnished newly completed pre-fabricated home in nearby Wealdstone, and contentedly sipped from their shared thermos of tea as the seats around them filled and the buzz of voices reverberated ever-louder in the great bowl of the old Empire – now Commonwealth – Stadium.

Greta had discovered at earlier England matches that when her husband got excited, the more he shouted the more Russian he sounded; and the more incongruous his near fanatical support for his adopted country seemed!

No matter, but for the madness of kings they might never have found each other in the first place!

The Portuguese had had no selection worries, with every man in the squad fit to play. Questions of systems and formations did not seem to trouble their Manager, forty-nine-year old Brazilian, Rio de Janeiro-born Otto Martins Glória, or Head Coach Manuel da Luz Afonso, who was the man who actually selected match teams. The two men had worked together at Benfica in the 1950s before Otto Glória had moved on to manage Belenenses, and Sporting Lisbon before going to France to coach Olympique de Marseille – where in his short stay he never lost a match – around the time of the October War. Afonso, meanwhile, had stayed in Lisbon and led Benfica to successive European Cup titles before the World went mad.

ENGLAND	NO.	PORTUGAL
G. Banks (Leicester City)	1	**J. Pereira** (Belenenses)
D. Howe (West Bromwich A.)	2	**A. Festa** (Porto)
J. Armfield (C) (Blackpool)	3	**A. Baptista** (Sporting Lisbon)
P. Swan (Sheffield Wednesday)	4	**J. Carlos** (Sporting Lisbon)
J. Charlton (Leeds United)	5	**Hilario** (Sporting Lisbon)
N. Stiles (Manchester United)	6	**J. Graca** (Vitória de Setúbal)
A. Ball (Blackpool)	7	**M. Coluna (C)** (Benfica)
N. Hunter (Leeds United)	8	**J. Augusto** (Benfica)
R. Charlton (Manchester United)	9	**Eusébio** (Benfica)
G. Hurst (Southampton)	10	**Torres** (Benfica)
B. Clough (Sunderland)	11	**A. Simões** (Benfica)

Picking a Portuguese side in that era was simply to write the names of Sporting Lisbon's best defenders at the top of the list and Benfica's forward line at the bottom. If there were any places left then there were a host of men from Belenenses, Porto, and Vitória de Setúbal to fill the gaps.

Benfica had been before the October War and nobody doubted still were, the best side in Europe, possibly Christendom and Sporting were only a little less formidable. Forget 4-3-3 or 4-4-2 or 4-2-4 or any of that nonsense, the game had been conceived as a 2-3-5 attacking feast: two full backs, a centre-half and two wing-backs who could defend or attack at need, and FIVE forwards. Portugal would play the Benfica way; three or four men at the back and everybody else laying siege to the opposition's goal!

Past results were no guide because Portugal had never fielded a side like this and Eusébio was, head and shoulders, obviously the best striker in world football at the moment.

The last time the two nations had met had been at Wembley in 1961 in a qualifying match for the Chile World Cup of 1962; and of the twenty-two men who had turned out on that night only six walked out onto the turf of the Commonwealth Stadium that afternoon. Armfield, Swan and Bobby Charlton for England; and Mario Coluna, Hilario and Eusébio for the Portuguese. England had won that last match two-nil. Arguably, while England were a match for the side Walter Winterbottom had coached back in 1961; indisputably *this* current Portugal team was an entirely different kettle of fish in comparison to the one which had flattered to deceive back in the fifties and early sixties.

The short build-up to the Final – only four days for England – had done little to tone down the hyperbole of Manchester's and Birmingham's reincarnated 'Fleet Streets' or the heat of the discussions which had, presumably raged in England's rapidly re-opening public houses.

The heart told most Englishmen who actually cared, probably a goodly percentage of the male population and surprisingly, of women also, that the Jules Rimet Trophy must be England's; nonetheless. the head had to admit, there was no two ways about it, that Portugal were by far the better all-round team.

It was a classic confrontation: English pluck, Agincourt all over again, set against the dazzling superiority of the foe. That said, not one of the Portuguese players believed that they were the favourites. England would never give up, the English were fit, solid in every department and in Hurst and Clough, Alf Ramsey had stumbled upon a workmanlike but undeniably effective goal-scoring duo. England would fight for every scrap of possession, keep running hard for the full ninety minutes and not fade in and out of the game like Brazil, and the Wembley roar would be like playing against two extra players if England got their noses in front.

Although there had been a hope that Prime Minister António de Oliveira Salazar might be persuaded – health permitting – to fly to England for the Final, on the actual day he was represented by the Portuguese Foreign Minister fifty-nine -year old Marcello José das Neves Alves Caetano, the man most foreign observers regarded as Salazar's natural successor if, or when the Portuguese leader decided to step down. Caetano was, like Salazar – with whom he enjoyed an allegedly 'tense' relationship - an academic turned politician currently in his third spell as Foreign Minister in Lisbon.

Caetano had swelled with pride as Margaret Thatcher had smiled and indicated that he should follow – ahead of her - in the Queen's wake as the Royal Party was presented to the players of the two sides.

The man Jimmy Armfield most remembered that day was 'the Colonel' the moustachioed, eyes twinkling with mischief, presence of the Prime Minister's former SAS-man husband bringing up the rear of the long line of dignitaries.

'For Queen and country!' He guffawed.

Armfield remembered other confidential asides, and struggled to keep a straight face, decades later in recollecting them.

'This is our bloody castle,' he said, waving around at the packed terraces and stands, 'nobody's going to take it from us!'

And 'just get stuck in chaps!'

'The Colonel stopped a moment to meet Cloughie's eye,' Armfield recalled with a shake of the head, 'they sized each other up and then, just nodded at each other as if to say *I've got your number, chum...*'

The England players were raring to go, unable to keep still. All except Brian Clough who was waiting, as cool as a cucumber as if he knew his moment had come and he meant to enjoy it, every single second of it.

'Good luck, Colonel," the Sunderland striker murmured as the old soldier moved on, nodding towards the Prime Minister who was, at that moment, shaking the hand of Portuguese Captain, Mario Coluna.

'I shall bloody well need it!' The older man chortled without missing a step.

'I wanted to elbow Cloughie in the ribs,' Armfield confessed. 'But then I realised the others were grinning like Cheshire cats and I knew that whatever happened in the next couple of hours the one thing we weren't going to do was freeze up with stage fright!'

Possibly, the most nervous man in the presentation line was the match referee, forty-five-year old Scotsman, Hugh Philips. Cynics later observed that the reason the Portuguese never raised any objection to Philips – an official from one of the British 'Home' Associations – was that a Scotsman was hardly likely to do the 'auld enemy' any favours. It is more likely that the Glória-Afonso partnership was simply mightily relieved that a reliable, firm hand was going to be in control of affairs that day at Wembley.

Philips had been on the Scottish Senior List of referees since 1951, officiating at several cup finals and international matches. He had refereed one of the group matches and run the line in one of the quarter-finals without attracting attention and it was known that he was not the sort of referee who would allow players to kick lumps out of each other.

Neither side was overly impressed by the choice of the two linesmen, Uruguayan José María Codesal, and Spaniard Juan Gardeazábal Garay; but this was the World Cup Final and it was only right and proper that there should be global representation at it!

Hugh Philips had already decided that he would hang up his whistle at the end of the tournament. To be awarded the Final was beyond a dream come true.

'I was quite prepared to send a man off if either side decided to cut up rough,' he claimed later. 'The World was watching us that day!"

Actually, that part of the world which gave a damn was more likely to be listening on longwave radios. The live television audience that day was estimated later as being around two million, all in the British Isles. Most people 'viewed' the Final through the filter of the words of BBC commentators Brian Moore, and when his voice failed him early in proceedings, by his colleague – former Reading and Northampton Town forward - Maurice Edelston. For the minority who had access to a working monochrome television set in an area which had a reliable electricity supply (at least during the course of that afternoon) the voice of the Final was to be Hugh Johns, recruited to the BBC a week before the tournament after a chance meeting with the then Director General David Attenborough, shortly before the latter finally escaped the 'curse of the DG's' seat and embarked on his life-long career documenting the natural world and its endless wonders for his fascinated and wondrously beguiled public.

Attenborough had originally pencilled in Barry Lankester, the presenter and producer of the immortal Battle of Malta and other documentaries for the Ministry of Information and the BBC as the star presenter and commentator to maximise the television audience. Lankester had never been very keen on this and had suggested several 'better qualified men', admitting many years later, to his chagrin, that he had not specifically mentioned Hugh Johns's name at that time.

'I had other projects in the go at the time and frankly, the World Cup did not seem that big a thing at the time.'

It is important to remember that the World Cup was viewed as an excuse for a party, for people to let off steam, not the initial engine of reconstruction it has become in popular memory.

C'est la vie...

Thus, nowadays in all the old film sequences it is Hugh Johns's alternately dulcet and exuberant tones which document the dramatic twists and turns of that never to be forgotten afternoon!

Jimmy Armfield won the toss and elected to attack the tunnel end of the great stadium; in the second half England would be advancing on a Portuguese goal framed by unbroken ramparts of terraces packed with a sea of Union Jacks.

Both sides lined up in their first-choice strips: England in white shirts, black-blue shorts and white socks; Portugal in Cardinal tops, white shorts and socks that matched their shirts. There was a breathless hush, Hugh Philips raised the whistle to his lips and with a shrill blast the game was afoot.

In the first minute Eusébio picked up the ball in the centre circle and Norman Hunter crashed into him like a bulldozer. If the Black Panther had wondered who was going to mark him that day the Leeds United destroyer had wasted no time giving him the first of numerous bruises and letting him know what he had to look forward to every time he was on the ball.

Referee Philips wagged his finger at Hunter.

Fifty years on the lunging tackle would have been a yellow card, or possibly, if the Referee had 'previous' with an offender, a straight red card. In July 1966 Hunter had not actually tried to kill the best player in the tournament, just let him know he was there.

Eusébio slowly picked himself up.

'Wherever he goes I want you breathing down his neck,' Alf Ramsey had instructed Norman Hunter. 'If you have trouble with the ref, we'll put Nobby [Stiles] on him but you're probably quicker than him, so you stick with it.'

Nobby Stiles was also a slighter man than the Leeds defender, and therefore conceivably easier for a man of Eusébio's bull-like strength to shrug off. No, it was much better to leave Hunter on the case, that way Stiles or Jack Charlton could pick up the pieces if Portugal's deadliest striker got away from the Leeds-man. Besides, Ramsey needed Stiles snapping at the heels of the other Portuguese stars, and harrying Mario Coluna in the middle of the park. The Portuguese side held threats all over the field; nobody could cover every base; all that could be hoped was that by harassing Coluna and negating – insofar as that was possible – Eusébio the smoothly-oiled goal-scoring machine which had brushed aside the Brazilians might be hobbled long enough for England to get home a telling blow at the other end of the pitch.

Five minutes later Eusébio side-stepped around Norman Hunter as if he was not there; *and* ran straight into Manchester United's pocket dynamo, Nobby Stiles, whom he literally fell over, sprawling at the feet of Jack Charlton.

'You weren't planning on going anywhere were you, lad?' The big man inquired, looking down grinning.

Not for the first time that afternoon Eusébio was baffled.

Jack Charlton never lost, or attempted to shrug off, his broad north-eastern accent. The Charltons were Ashington-born, the children of a Northumberland mining community and fiercely proud of it.

The Panther had no idea what the giraffe-like centre-half was actually saying to him, other than that it was a question of some kind but man to man, footballer to footballer, he understood *exactly* what the elder Charlton brother *meant*.

25 | They Think It's All Over!

All the players on the field that day had played in matches where the tackles started at waist high and got higher. There were no angels in international or domestic football. Given the stakes the Final might easily have turned into one of those sort of brutal games; that it did not was possibly the highest tribute that could be paid to the twenty-two gladiators, especially those in the red shirts of Portugal. The Englishmen were the ones who set the tone; competing for the ball with a deliberate, sustained ferocity knowing that a tiny misjudgement would send an opponent spinning or thudding to the floor and invite retaliation. There was no retaliation, other than in kind. Hard but fair does not do it justice. *Very* hard and *sometimes* borderline violent albeit mostly fair – by the lights of the time - probably does that riveting counter-punching first half due credit.

Listen again to Brian Moore's and Maurice Edelston's radio commentary, or Hugh Johns on TV; you can feel them wincing as the tackles flew in, some a fraction early, others late, the majority timed to perfection.

'It was painful to watch,' Moore smiled twenty years later, 'but it was compelling. There were no cheap shots, everything was face to face, real men standing toe to toe and the Portuguese, who played the better football throughout understood that if they wanted to express their talents they were going to have to fight like, well...Panthers.'

The first goal came against the run of play in the twenty-seventh minute after Mario Coluna had body-checked Bobby Charlton thirty yards out and about twenty yards in from the left touchline. Norman Hunter and Don Howe argued about who should take the free kick and the Leeds man shrugged, appeared to turn away before taking two steps and clipping the ball on a low trajectory, hardly head height towards the near corner of the six-yard box. Geoff Hurst got his head to the ball – he always seemed to get his head to the ball if it was anywhere near him – nodding it down directly at the goalkeeper's feet. Pereira was only two to three yards away, too close to react, the ball looped off his shin and quick as a flash Brian Clough and two defenders had bundled the ball, in a blur of bodies into the back of the net.

'It went in off my knee,' Clough always claimed.

All subsequent analysis suggested it went in either off his left, or Alberto Festa's right forearm, or both at the same time. The BBC did not show replays at the time, let alone have the facility to resort to ultra-slow motion to comprehensively settle such matters. In any event the surviving film footage is too grainy – and from completely the wrong angle – to help anybody and therefore settles absolutely nothing.

For posterity the record book shows that Brian Clough scored the first goal of the 1966 World Cup Final!

It was to be only the first of many controversies that still ring down the years whenever talk turns to 'the great match'. Oddly, the discussion often fails to mention that Alf Ramsey, in bringing in Norman Hunter on the left of midfield had stumbled upon the perfect way to balance his side. What England lost in creativity was more than compensated for by the new resilience of the team in front of the back four, which, Peter Swan apart was relatively pedestrian in international terms. Moreover, in losing Ron Flowers's distributive skills and goal threat much greater responsibility now fell on Bobby Charlton's shoulders, and with both Nobby Stiles and Norman Hunter effectively acting as his minders, 'our Bobby' began to carry the ball forward, and every time he received the ball there was a murmur of excitement, anticipation. Suddenly the ball was regularly curving out to the wing or finding Geoff Hurst on the edge of the penalty box, or Charlton was causing panic as he carried the ball forward into shooting range; so, while theoretically, England had less options in fact they had fewer but *better* ones!

Notwithstanding, it was a rare loose pass in his own half in the last minute of the first half which allowed Eusébio to put his Benfica striking partner José Torres through, one on one with the last defender, Peter Swan. A rangy, powerful six feet three inches tall the Benfica faithful called Torres *O Bom Gigante* - the Kind Giant – and in a moment he had forged past Peter Swan into the box, latched onto Eusébio's through ball and struck like a viper from a dozen yards out.

Impossibly, Gordon Banks got the tips of the fingers of his left hand to the missile, perhaps deflecting its flight by an inch or so; sufficient for it to crash into the underside of the crossbar adjacent to England's left-hand goalpost rather than to fly unobstructed into the net. As fast as, or faster than the human eye could discern the ball dove behind the still prostrate Banks, to whose horror the ball struck.

'I felt it clout me on the right hip and I thought...bugger, that must be going in now...'

Torres could not believe he had not scored with his initial strike and neither could anybody else, and when Don Howe slid in to intercept the ball as it seemed it must trickle into the net off Gordon Banks's rump the stunned sigh of relief all around the huge stadium was palpable.

It tells us a lot about the sophistication of broadcasting in England in that age that it was not until the next day when BBC technicians began to pore over the tapes of the previous day's live broadcast, that it was belatedly recognised that the referee had been wrong to wave away Eusébio's and José Simões's impassioned pleas for a goal to be awarded. Hugh Philips, his line of sight obscured by Banks and Howe, and with the nearest linesman over thirty yards behind the play, had not seen the ball cross the line a split second before Don Howe's despairing clearance.

The guilty look on Don Howe's face as he picked himself up from the back of the net gives it all away in those old, grainy frames. The ball had dribbled over the line and by the time Howe got a boot to it there was clear air between the goal line and the ball.

Referee Philips had shrugged and spread his arms wide.

'I'm sorry, boys,' he explained to the Portuguese players. 'I honestly couldn't see if it went over the line and I can't give what I can't see!'

Several of the Portuguese understood and spoke some if not a lot of English but inevitably, in the heat of the moment a great deal probably gets lost in translation.

At the half-time whistle Mario Coluna wrapped his arms around Simões and dragged him away to stop him stalking the referee and his linesmen down the tunnel.

Understandably, the injustice of that goal that never was spurred on the visitors. For fifteen minutes – the longest spell either side was really on top that afternoon – Portugal flowed forward in languid, elegant waves in attacks that ended with lightning flourishes. Three, four times Gordon Banks blocked or stopped goal bound rockets before in the fifty-ninth minute José Torres outjumped Jack Charlton at the far post and finally levelled the scores.

Geoff Hurst and Brian Clough had been spectators in the second-half until then. Yet within sixty seconds of the kick-off the Portuguese were walking around asking each other: '*O que acabou de acontecer?*

WHAT JUST HAPPENED?

What had JUST happened was that Bobby Charlton had carried the ball out of the centre circle, jinking this way and that, slid a pass to Alan Ball as he cut in from the right wing, and his cross, dipping into the middle of the box had been intercepted by Geoff Hurst, whereupon the striker had turned, fired in a shot blocked by Alberto Festa and Brian Clough, with the icy clear-headed touch of a footballing assassin had smashed the ball past José Pereira's right shoulder from point blank range.

The Portuguese looked to Uruguayan linesman José María Codesal, as they had in the first-half to right the wrong of the denial of Torres's goal, appealing for an offside flag that stayed resolutely down. Since Geoff Hurst's shot had come off Festa it could not have been offside but in a just world Senior Codesal would have waved his flag and one injustice at least might have been cancelled out by another.

Briefly, Portugal lost their composure and their shape and their raggedness and anger, as often happens, also infected the Englishmen. Jimmy Armfield found himself exposed, alone on the left twenty yards out as Eusébio and Simões swept past him and suddenly José Augusto, the twenty-nine-year old Benfica star who might have been the most famous Portuguese footballer of his age but for the phenomena that was Eusébio, slid the ball past Gordon Banks with casual aplomb.

That was when the on-field England 'brains trust' – Armfield, Howe and Jack Charlton – met, caught their collective breaths and decided that 'this headless chicken stuff isn't going to do us any good!'

The next time England got the ball they held onto it and invited the Portuguese to get it back, slowing the game, allowing nerves to settle and men bamboozled and a little disorientated by Portugal's scintillating second half twenty minutes to remember what they were supposed to be doing.

Four men across the back, four in midfield with Geoff Hurst playing in a slightly withdrawn position behind the predatory Clough up front. That was the plan; perhaps, it is time we started following it again?

Portuguese incursions into England territory began to founder on the unyielding rocks of the elder Charlton and his more mobile partner, Swan.

Alf Ramsey had always regarded Peter Swan as the best all-round defender in the country; not only was he a granite-like anchor in the heart of the defence, he was confident on the ball, capable of carrying and passing not simply pummelling the ball upfield. In the modern game the long ball habits of the past were rapidly becoming meat and drink to organised defences; the future lay with men who could carry or pass the ball out of defence. Norman Hunter was a player in the same mould, although at Leeds his manager, Don Revie, preferred to use him in the 'stopper' or 'hard-man enforcer' role.

It had been the hallmark of Ramsey's success at Ipswich Town to get the very best out of men discarded or under-valued by other coaches or former teams, to see things in players that others either did not see or had under-valued. Now that he had the best players in the country at his disposal looking to get the best out of them must have been a joy in those early days of his reign.

Norman Hunter never played for England – other than on a few specific occasions, such as in the Argentina Semi-final – in his Leeds United mode. Likewise, Alan Ball under Ramsey's tutelage turned into an English version of Mario Coluna over the years, and Nobby Stiles eventually became as much the England side's talisman as he was the non-stop reliable defensive midfielder, he was in 1966.

But all that lay in an unknown and unknowable future that day in July beneath a sun that beat down on a sweltering Commonwealth Stadium as if it was the first day of the summer of a new age.

Both sides had goals disallowed within minutes.

First Geoff Hurst was ruled offside leaping to head a Bobby Charlton near post cross past Pereira; but only after Senior Codesal had flagged so posthumously that most of the England team had already swarmed forward to congratulate the would-be scorer.

Eusébio mistimed his run by a fraction in the seventy-third minute; this time Spanish linesman Juan Gardeazábal Garay signalled with alacrity and the referee's whistle blew as the ball evaded Gordon Banks.

Both offside calls have been endlessly studied.

Both were as 'marginal' as each other, of the two Hurst seemed to be more 'level' with the last defender than Eusébio. Sport at the highest level is always a matter of the narrowest of hair-thin 'margins'. That day both sides were treading a razor's edge.

Tiring men summoned their last reserves of strength, launched into last gasp tackles, trudged into position, forced themselves to chase every lost cause.

Six minutes remained on the clock when Geoff Hurst chased a ball to the goal line a yard outside the Portuguese penalty box and to his, and defender Alexandre da Silva Baptista's – his calves cramping with his socks rolled down around his ankles – surprise the England number ten reached the ball in time to clip it diagonally back across the box.

'I saw it – visualised it, people say now - whizzing into the top corner before I actually hit it,' Brian Clough claimed in later years. 'Mind you if the ball had bobbled or the keeper had closed down the angle, or one of the defenders had anticipated Geoff getting to the line, *visualising* scoring the goal wouldn't have helped a lot. But it sat up nicely for me and I was always going to put it into the top right-hand corner!"

Once more Wembley erupted in a paroxysm of celebration.

Around the field Portuguese heads dropped.

In their exuberance scores of fans spilled off the terraces at each end of the Commonwealth Stadium and began to press against the barriers – these were the temporary improvised 'crash' or 'crush' barriers hastily erected after the pitch invasion in the Argentina match -

behind each goal.

Policemen and stewards began to move into position, around the Royal Box the men of the Prime Minister's Royal Marines AWP, and the Queen's faithful Black Watch fingered the trigger guards of their SLRs.

'They think it's all over!' Brian Moore croaked; his voice so strained he had handed over to his radio colleague Maurice Edelston at the start of the second-half before reclaiming the microphone around the eightieth minute of the match. He pointed at the spectators starting to pour onto the turf where the old dog-racing cinder track had been before the war.

'There are people close to the pitch!' Edelston complained, so focused on the action he had eyes for nothing but the ball as the Portuguese kicked off yet again. 'Can England hold out?'

Mario Coluna waved all his men forward.

Portugal Head Coach Manuel da Luz Afonso ran from the bench and began gesticulating at his men from the side lines to throw caution to the wind, counting down the minutes with upheld fingers.

Four minutes…

José Augusto's left-foot shot took a deflection off Jimmy Armfield's hip and hit Gordon Banks in the face before he could react. The ball scuttled behind for a corner.

The Portuguese coach waved for goalkeeper José Pereira to sprint upfield; Brian Clough tracked back with him leaving two thirds of the pitch empty.

Simões swung in a corner which dipped towards the penalty spot and a dozen bodies converged on it with a commitment that verged on suicidal recklessness. The ball cannoned around like a pinball as feet flailed at it, ricocheting off shins before Banks fell on it, smothered it and clutched it to his chest.

Wembley breathed again.

Pereira turned and sprinted back towards his own half.

All around him men were yelling at Banks to boot the ball upfield where Geoff Hurst, Brian Clough and Alan Ball were competing to get into the Portugal half first.

Clough pulled up with cramp as he crossed the centre line, collapsing in agony just inside the Portugal half.

Meanwhile Geoff Hurst, the Southampton man lagged a few yards behind the apparently inexhaustible red-headed Blackpool winger.

Gordon Banks belatedly realised that there was a fleeting opportunity to kill off the game and hoofed the ball as hard as he could upfield in an attempt to find the England runners.

The ball bounced high five yards inside the Portugal half, Hurst and Festa fought for it and suddenly Alan Ball was streaking after it trying to get it under control before José Pereira got between him and his empty, seductively inviting goal.

'I could feel my calves seizing up with cramp,' Ball said, 'it was like trying to run through mud except a lot more painful. In the end I couldn't make up my mind whether to chip the keeper – I was thirty-five or forty yards out and he hadn't even got back into his box – or lay the ball back for Geoff or Cloughie. I had no idea Brian was rolling around on the floor by then. In the end I didn't do either, I just thumped the ball; scuffed it, to tell the truth, and fell over. I heard the crowd jump up and cheer, and suddenly go quiet. Geoff had got on the end of the shot I'd completely miss hit and thumped it into the crowd. the ball was off the pitch for what seemed like hours...'

Geoff Hurst had actually missed an open goal from eighteen yards out.

Two minutes left on the clock.

In the sixties, referees were notoriously disinclined to add extra minutes to a half to compensate for delays, stoppages and injuries. When the ninety minutes of the match expired; that would be that bar a few token seconds.

Geoff Hurst picked himself up off the turf, and soon caught up with Alan Ball painfully limping and hopping back towards the England end. Brian Clough was still on the ground as José Pereira galloped past him again.

Those last seconds stretched as time seemed to slow down; and then virtually stop.

Don Howe brought down Simões a yard outside the angle of the box, England's walking wounded were pushed into a wall, and near the penalty spot Jack Charlton, Norman Hunter and Peter Swan wrestled and barged the nearest man in a red shirt, Jimmy Armfield and Don Howe stood on the goal line guarding each post.

Time was up.

On the England bench Alf Ramsey sat impassively as all around him squad players, coaches and a clump of Football Association and Organising Committee men were on their feet pleading for the final whistle.

Nobody had really believed that England, weakened by the loss of a third of its professional footballers in the October War, and after a preparation comprising three internationals against the Home Countries and a handful of practice matches that spring and summer, would get this far let alone be leading in the World Cup Final as the last seconds ticked away.

Except perhaps, Ramsey himself.

Now as he was about to be vindicated, the man who had been England Manager in name alone for three-and-a-half years before the national side's return to competition that February against Scotland gave every appearance of being by far and away the calmest man in the Commonwealth Stadium as José Simões's curling free kick whipped into England's heavily congested penalty area.

Eusébio – who else? – rose through the crowd of shoulders and elbows and met the ball with his forehead. The contact point was approximately a yard to the left of the penalty spot and the ball flew like a bullet low to Gordon Banks's right hand.

The England goalkeeper hurled himself across his goal line.

Everybody knew, intuitively, there was absolutely nothing he could do about it...right until the ball struck his right wrist and flew up, and over the crossbar!

26 | Epilogue

A historian will tell you that the World Cup of 1966 was 'a blip, an outlier, one of those things that makes one feel good about oneself and one's country but which otherwise, has little lasting impact on the fate of nations.'

I am fairly confident that I am not the only one who thinks it is not history that is 'bunk'; but certain historians! Yes, all that happened was that England became World Champions and new sporting myths and legends were born. No, the woes of the world continued unabated in 1966 and undeniably, got worse thereafter.

At the time the man in the street in the United Kingdom had no real idea what was going on in America, or the mendacity under-pinning the Sino-Soviet alliance and what it might mean for what was left of western Europe. Closer to home new troubles were brewing in the Mediterranean and France, and while Franco fulminated against what he saw as the 'historic betrayal of Portugal', the possibility of a new war with Spain could never be discounted in those years.

Let it not be forgotten that there was no formal 'ceasefire' in the South Atlantic, and that Argentina had competed in England while technically, still at war with the United Kingdom. All of which makes it all the more remarkable that the main reason Margaret Thatcher's Government backed and made possible the staging of the 1966 tournament was not to stop the South Americans – Argentina mainly – hijacking the World Cup but to kick start the generational project of post-October War reconstruction.

Those who say this was symbolic, tokenistic and that the real reconstruction did not get under way until the early 1970s, miss the point. There was no real impetus for general reconstruction – just various planning exercises and forums – before the summer of 1966; afterwards, the British people actually took promises of reclaiming the ruins seriously. Re-building new Jerusalems from the wreckage of the old world was pie in the sky before July 1966; afterwards it was the great national project that underwrote every government – of whatever political hue – for the rest of the century.

So, what of the heroes of Wembley that day in July 1966?

Well, that is the subject of another book; but not right now or for a while yet.

That World Cup winning team never played together again. Suffice to say that several men retired to take up 'proper jobs' soon after the 'hullabaloo quietened down', others went on to illustrious playing and managerial careers in the game. More than one of the 'winners' became national treasures.

Let me leave you with a quote from the lips of one such, delivered during an interview with Brian Moore over thirty years later on a dark, windy night in the English Midlands after his side had lost at home to, of all teams, Benfica.

'That's all very well for you to say,' he retorted blithely. 'I'm fed up with people on TV and in the press criticising me and my players because we can't walk on water!'

'Yes, we know that, but...'

'No buts. I'll tell you what I tell my lads when they start acting as if they know it all.' At this point the great man's audience would be on the edge of their seats, ready to chorus the punchline in unison. 'Don't think you can tell me anything I don't already know. Don't forget that I'm the man who scored the goals that won the World Cup, lad!'

[The End]

Appendix 1 | The England Squad

The England Squad selected for the 1966 World Cup Finals in the 10/27/62 timeline.

Age on 2/7/66– Full name (Date of Birth), Team

Goalkeepers
30 - Ronald Deryk George Springett (22/7/35), Sheffield Wednesday
29 - Alan Hodgkinson (16/8/36), Sheffield United
28 - Gordon Banks (30/12/37) Leicester City

Defenders & Defensive Midfielders
30 - James Christopher Armfield (21/9/35) Blackpool
30 - Donald Howe (12/10/35) West Bromwich Albion
23 - Norbert Peter 'Nobby' Stiles (18/5/42) Manchester United
22 - Bobby Thomson (5/12/43) Wolverhampton Wanderers
25 - Keith Robert Newton (23/6/41) Blackburn Rovers
31 - John 'Jack' Charlton (8/5/35) Leeds United
22 - Norman Hunter (29/10/43) Leeds United
29 - Peter Swan (8/10/36) Sheffield Wednesday
29 - Gerald Morton Young (1/10/36) Sheffield Wednesday

Midfielders
31 - Ronald Flowers (28/7/34) Wolverhampton Wanderers
28 - Robert 'Bobby' Charlton (11/10/37) Manchester United
23 - Michael O'Grady (11/10/42) Huddersfield Town)
21 - Peter Eustace (31/7/44) Sheffield Wednesday

Wingers
26 - Terry Lionel Paine (23/3/39) Southampton
21 - Alan Ball (12/5/45) Blackpool

Forwards
24 - Geoffrey Charles Hurst (8/12/41) Southampton
27 - John Michael Connelly (18/7/38) Burnley

31 - Derek Tennyson Kevan (6/3/35) West Bromwich Albion
31 - Brian Howard Clough (21/3/35) Sunderland

Appendix 2 | A Note on Players

A note on the three players included in 'FOOTBALL IN THE RUINS' whose careers ended prematurely **after** 27th October 1962 in the timeline in which **we actually live today**; or who missed the World Cup of 1966 **in our timeline** as a result of injury.

In our timeline **Brian Clough's** career as a professional footballer was pretty much ended on 26th December 1962 when he suffered a medial cruciate ligament injury – playing for Sunderland at Roker Park - in a collision with Bury goalkeeper Chris Harker.

In the post-Cuban Missiles War era there was no league football played in England between 28th October 1962 and the beginning of the 1963-64 Season in late August 1963.

Brian Clough did not therefore suffer a career-ending injury in the altered timeline of the 10/27/62 world and continued to pursue his footballing career until the 1967/68 season.

In our timeline **Donald 'Don' Howe** missed out on selection to Alf Ramsay's 1966 World Cup squad because in March of that year he broke his leg playing for Arsenal against Blackpool.

In our timeline Howe only joined Arsenal from West Bromwich Albion in 1964. In the 10/27/62 timeline Howe never played for Arsenal.

In our timeline **Peter Swan** was banned from football for life years on 13th April 1964 for his involvement in a betting scandal.

In the altered 10/27/62 timeline he was not implicated in a career-ending scandal of any kind.

In my narrative of the altered 10/27/62 timeline the following players selected in Alf Ramsey's **actual** World

Cup winning squad *in our timeline* did not survive, died later, or went missing during, shortly thereafter or in the period 28th October 1962 to 31st December 1965.

Bonetti, Peter Phillip (Chelsea)
Byrne, Gerald 'Gerry' (Liverpool)
Callaghan, Ian Robert (Liverpool)
Cohen, George Reginald (Fulham)
Eastham, George Edward (Fulham)
Greaves, James Peter 'Jimmy' (Tottenham Hotspur)
Hunt, Roger (Liverpool)
Moore, Robert 'Bobby' (West Ham United)
Peters, Martin Stanford (West Ham United)
Wilson, Ramon 'Ray' (Everton)

Finally, a number of Scottish and Welsh players who played for London or Liverpool-based teams in 1966 appear in FOOTBALL IN THE RUINS for their respective national teams.

ALL of these men played for teams outside of the bombed/devastated cities, towns and locales hit during the Cuban Missiles War on the night of 27/28th October 1962 (that is, in Scotland or areas of England or Wales not directly targeted in the events which caused the 10/27/62 timeline to diverge from the one in which we actually live today).

It goes without saying that the author apologises profusely to his readers for the tautological mental somersaults inherent in the above notes!

JP.
(June 2018)

Appendix 3 | Match List

The World Cup – 1966: Chronology

GROUP MATCHES

England 1-1 Chile
4/7/66 – Wembley, (Commonwealth Stadium)
Att. 98,500
Goals: **England** – J. Charlton (87); **Chile** – Marcos (6)

Brazil 4-1 Switzerland
5/7/66 – Sheffield (Hillsborough)
Att. 33,943
Goals: **Brazil** – Garrincha (14), Pelé (36, 55), Tostão
(79); **Switzerland** – Gottardi (85)

Argentina 1-0 Sweden
5/7/66 – Manchester (Old Trafford)
Att. 29,508
Goals: **Argentina** – Mas (58)

Portugal 3-1 Colombia
5/7/66 – Middlesbrough (Ayresome Park)
Att. 27,971
Goals: **Portugal** – Jose Augusto (47), Simões (54) Jose
Carlos (57); **Colombia** – Gamboa (29)

Spain 6-0 Ghana
6/7/66 – Wembley (Commonwealth Stadium)
Att. 23,860
Goals: **Spain** – Gento (41, 56, 84), Pirri (48), Amancio
(59, 71)

Scotland 0-0 Mexico
6/7/66 – Birmingham (Villa Park)
Att. 46,412

Uruguay 0-0 Wales
6/7/66 – Leeds (Elland Road)
Att. 34,003
Sent Off: **Uruguay** – Troche (66)

Italy 2-0 Northern Ireland
6/7/66 – Sunderland (Roker Park)
Att. 38,118
Goals: **Italy** – Rivera (32), Mazzola (51)

Ghana 0-4 Chile
8/7/66 – West Ham (Upton Park)
Att. 21,078
Goals: **Chile** – Campos (11), Toro (39, 62), Moreno (51)

Brazil 2-2 Scotland
8/7/66 – Sheffield (Hillsborough)
Att. 35,779
Goals: **Brazil** – Zito (25), Pelé (68); **Scotland** – Law (55), Gilzean (88)

Argentina 1-0 Wales
8/7/66 – Manchester (Old Trafford)
Att. 31,906
Goals: **Argentina** – Mas (72)

Portugal 2-1 Italy
8/7/66 – Middlesbrough (Ayresome park)
Att. 28.657
Goals: **Portugal** – Eusébio (72), Coluna (78); **Italy** – Rivera (89)

England 2-1 Spain
9/7/66 – Wembley (Commonwealth Stadium)
Att. 96,156
Goals: **England** – Connelly (49), Kevan (74); **Spain** – Amancio (34)

Mexico 1-1 Switzerland
9/7/66 – Birmingham (Villa Park)
Att. 22,389
Goals: **Mexico** – Borja (37); **Switzerland** – Quentin (67)

Sweden 0-1 Uruguay
9/7/66 – Leeds (Elland Road)
Att. 19,408
Goals: **Uruguay** – Rocha (48)

Colombia 1-2 Northern Ireland
9/7/66 – Sunderland (Roker Park)
Att. 37,106
Goals: **Colombia** – Elder *OG* (80); **Northern Ireland** –
Best (58), Crossan (82)

England 9-0 Ghana
12/7/66 – Wembley (Commonwealth Stadium)
Att. 88,744
Goals: **England** – Hurst (23, 26 34, 58, 73, 89), J.
Charlton (61), Connelly (77), B. Charlton (85)

Mexico 1-4 Brazil
12/7/66 – Sheffield (Hillsborough)
Att. 33,394
Goals: **Mexico** – Reyes (86); **Brazil** – Pelé (15), Jairzinho
(22, 66), Garrincha (52)

Argentina 0-0 Uruguay
12/7/66 – Leeds (Elland Road)
Att. 24,702

Portugal 4-1 Northern Ireland
12/7/66 – Sunderland (Roker Park)
Att. 35,881
Goals: **Portugal** – Eusébio (6, 18, 29), Coluna (60);
Northern Ireland – Crossan (70)

Spain 3-1 Chile
13/7/66 – West Ham (Upton Park)
Att. 19,148
Goals: **Spain** – Amancio (9, 15), Pirri (68); **Chile** – Toro
(33)

Scotland 2-1 Switzerland
13/7/66 – Birmingham (Villa Park)
Att. 43,125
Goals: **Scotland** – Gilzean (60), Cooke (65); **Switzerland**
– Gottardi *Pen* (40)

Sweden 2-3 Wales
13/7/66 – Manchester (Old Trafford)

Att. 30,852
Goals: **Sweden** – (Henry) Larsson (18, 75); **Wales** – W. Davies (13, 62), R. Davies (74)

Italy 3-0 Colombia
13/7/66 – Middlesbrough (Ayresome Park)
Att. 23,724
Goals: **Italy** – Mazzola (43, 71), Rivera *Pen* (63)

QUARTER-FINALS

Played on 16/7/66.

England 4-3 Scotland (AET: 2-2 at FT)
Wembley (Commonwealth Stadium)
98,303
Goals: **England** – B. Charlton (14, 99), Flowers (56), Clough (117); **Scotland** – Gilzean (18, 93), Law (87)

Argentina 2-1 Italy (AET: 1-1 at FT)
Sheffield (Hillsborough)
Att. 33,788
Goals: **Argentina** – Onega *Pen* (85), Mas (90); **Italy** – Rivera *Pen* (53)
Sent Off: **Argentina** – Marzolini (53); **Italy** – Facchetti (85)

Brazil 3-1 Spain
Birmingham (Villa Park)
Att. 41,207
Goals: **Brazil** – Tostão (49), Pelé (61), Gerson (64); **Spain** – Pirri (39)

Portugal 5-0 Uruguay
Sunderland (Roker Park)
Att. 36,004
Goals: **Portugal** – Eusébio (32), Torres (51, 61, 70), Simões (75)
Sent Off: **Uruguay** – Rocha (27)

SEMI FINALS

Brazil 2-3 Portugal

18/7/66 – Birmingham (Villa Park)

Att. 44,554

Goals: **Brazil** – Pelé (59), Jairzinho (70); **Portugal** – Eusébio (48), Torres (53, 79)

England 3-0 Argentina

19/7/66 – Wembley (Commonwealth Stadium)

Att. 97,887

Goals: **England** – Clough (72), Hurst (78, 89)

Sent Off: **Argentina** – Varacka (78)

THIRD PLACE PLAY OFF MATCH

Argentina v. Brazil

22/7/66 – Wembley (Commonwealth Stadium)

Argentina disqualified for failure to fulfil fixture.

Brazil awarded 3rd Place in World Rankings.

WORLD CUP FINAL

England 3-2 Portugal

23/7/66 – Wembley (Commonwealth Stadium)

98,479

Goals: **England** – Clough (27, 59, 84); **Portugal** – Torres (58), Augusto (68)

Author's Endnote

'Football in the Ruins – The World Cup of 1966' is a standalone book in the alternative history series **Timeline 10/27/62**. I hope you enjoyed it - or if you did not, sorry - but either way, thank you for reading and helping to keep the printed word alive. Remember, civilization depends on people like you.

———————

Oh, please bear in mind that:

Inevitably, in writing an alternative history this book has referenced, attributed motives, actions and put words in the mouths of real, historical characters.

No motive, action or word attributed to a real person after 27th October 1962 actually happened or was said.

Whereas, to the best of my knowledge everything in this book which occurred before 27th October 1962 actually happened!

Other Books by James Philip

New England Series

Book 1: Empire Day
Book 2: Two Hundred Lost Years
Book 3: Travels Through the Wind
Book 4: Remember Brave Achilles
Book 5: George Washington's Ghost
Book 6: The Imperial Crisis
Book 7: The Lines of Laredo

The River Hall Chronicles

Book 1: Things Can Only Get Better
Book 2: Consenting Adults
Book 3: All Swing Together
Book 4: The Honourable Member

The Guy Winter Mysteries

Prologue: Winter's Pearl
Book 1: Winter's War
Book 2: Winter's Revenge
Book 3: Winter's Exile
Book 4: Winter's Return
Book 5: Winter's Spy
Book 6: Winter's Nemesis

The Bomber War Series

Book 1: Until the Night
Book 2: The Painter
Book 3: The Cloud Walkers

Until the Night Series

Part 1: Main Force Country – September 1943
Part 2: The Road to Berlin – October 1943
Part 3: The Big City – November 1943

Part 4: When Winter Comes – December 1943
Part 5: After Midnight – January 1944

The Harry Waters Series

Book 1: Islands of No Return
Book 2: Heroes
Book 3: Brothers in Arms

The Frankie Ransom Series

Book 1: A Ransom for Two Roses
Book 2: The Plains of Waterloo
Book 3: The Nantucket Sleighride

The Strangers Bureau Series

Book 1: Interlopers
Book 2: Pictures of Lily

James Philip's Cricket Books

F.S. Jackson
Lord Hawke

Cricket Books edited by James Philip

The James D. Coldham Series
[Edited by James Philip]

Books

Northamptonshire Cricket: A History [1741-1958]
Lord Harris

Anthologies

Volume 1: Notes & Articles
Volume 2: Monographs No. 1 to 8

Monographs

No. 1 - William Brockwell
No. 2 - German Cricket
No. 3 - Devon Cricket
No. 4 - R.S. Holmes
No. 5 - Collectors & Collecting
No. 6 - Early Cricket Reporters
No. 7 – Northamptonshire
No. 8 - Cricket & Authors

———

Details of all James Philip's published books and forthcoming publications can be found on his website
www.jamesphilip.co.uk

———

Cover artwork concepts by James Philip
Graphic Design by
Beastleigh Web Design